Pride Publis

Si
The Drumbeat of His Heart
A Song for His Heart
Karma's Kiss
Greedy Boy
Feral Woods

It's a Kink Thing
Kinked Up
Unkinked
Kinks and Crosshairs
Dupli-Kinked
Getting Kinky
On Kink's Edge

Collections
Secret Santa: Daddy's Secret
All Hallow's Harem: Candy Magic

Secret Santa

DADDY'S SECRET

M.C. ROTH

Daddy's Secret
ISBN # 978-1-80250-570-2
©Copyright M.C. Roth 2022
Cover Art by Kelly Martin ©Copyright December 2022
Interior text design by Claire Siemaszkiewicz
Pride Publishing

This is a work of fiction. All characters, places and events are from the author's imagination and should not be confused with fact. Any resemblance to persons, living or dead, events or places is purely coincidental.

All rights reserved. No part of this publication may be reproduced in any material form, whether by printing, photocopying, scanning or otherwise without the written permission of the publisher, Pride Publishing.

Applications should be addressed in the first instance, in writing, to Pride Publishing. Unauthorised or restricted acts in relation to this publication may result in civil proceedings and/or criminal prosecution.

The author and illustrator have asserted their respective rights under the Copyright Designs and Patents Acts 1988 (as amended) to be identified as the author of this book and illustrator of the artwork.

Published in 2022 by Pride Publishing, United Kingdom.

No part of this book may be reproduced, scanned, or distributed in any printed or electronic form without permission. Please do not participate in or encourage piracy of copyrighted materials in violation of the authors' rights. Purchase only authorised copies.

Pride Publishing is an imprint of Totally Entwined Group Limited.

If you purchased this book without a cover you should be aware that this book is stolen property. It was reported as "unsold and destroyed" to the publisher and neither the author nor the publisher has received any payment for this "stripped book".

DADDY'S SECRET

Dedication

For Q

Chapter One

"Excuse me." Sullivan took a step back, sucking in his stomach to let Debbie pass him. She gave him a sweet smile on her way, her reindeer earrings flashing between red and green. They were adorable cartoonish decorations that weighed her lobes down so much that the holes stretched.

I'll have to ask her where she got those. He didn't have any visible piercings, but he had a few fun places to dangle a flashing Christmas tree ornament. The only problem would be if the heavy thing caught on his shirt. If that happened, it was bye-bye nipples.

The area was packed with employees who he'd barely seen for the entire year. At the first sign of food and presents, they'd all pushed out of their offices to congregate in the largest boardroom. *Jingle Bells* played in the background, but even with the volume cranked, he could scarcely hear it over the din of conversation.

It was hard to believe how much the company had grown. When he'd started at the office, there had been a mishmash of twenty employees who had given multitasking a whole new meaning, and while their numbers had multiplied, the outdated boardrooms had stayed the same.

"Can I have your attention, folks?" Samantha shouted while perching on the edge of a stationary office chair. She was tiny, but her voice carried across the room and cut through every conversation with the same sharpness as her four-inch heels.

Sullivan wasn't sure how she managed it. He could bellow and one person in twenty might give him a second look, but she only had to whisper and she had every ear. Maybe she was just scarier than he was.

"First off, Merry Christmas, and thank you all so much for taking the time to participate in this year's Secret Santa." She wobbled on the chair before sending Sullivan a winning smile. "I know we have a lot of new faces this year, and this has always been one way to help make everyone feel welcomed."

A touch of warmth settled into Sullivan's stomach. Five years ago, he'd single-handedly started up a social committee for the company, and since then, he'd made more friends than he could count. Work was, well...*work*, but he tried his best to keep people wanting to come back every day.

The first year of Secret Santa had been an overwhelming success, with nearly everyone signing up. After that, it had almost become mandatory...like taxes.

"I think I'll get Sully and Mark to hand out gifts to everyone, and you're all welcome to mingle as long as you'd like. Just a reminder that the office will be closing down for Christmas break soon, but I'll see you back in a few weeks, broke and sober." There were a few awkward chuckles before silence fell.

Crap. Sullivan face-palmed. Samantha was four years sober, and she still made the worst drunk jokes he'd ever heard. She *thought* they were funny, too, which was the worst part.

Time to play savior.

He rushed to the front of the room before she could start speaking again, parking himself next to the tree and reaching out to stabilize her with one hand as she started to lose her balance.

The tree was a glorious thing that he'd carted all the way from the lot and through the front doors. The needles had been a disaster, sticking in every bit of carpeting and stabbing people at random when they insisted on only wearing socks.

There were over sixty gifts underneath it, most decently wrapped and a few in brightly colored bags. The only eyesore was the T-shirt that had a piece of tape on it with a name. Whoever had left it hadn't bothered to wrap it.

Reaching around the back of the tree, he pulled out his stash of emergency bags and slid the T-shirt inside one of them. Every year there was someone who didn't get a gift or a proper wrap job, and he'd learned early on to keep a secondary plan in place.

Helping Samantha down from the chair, he grabbed the first gift, reading the tag carefully before handing it off to Mark. As the pile went down, he had to point off into the crowd and call a few names, showing Mark the way as he stumbled. The guy tried so hard, but he was terrible with names and faces.

The crowd slowly dispersed as the gifts went out, leaving some breathing room as the temperature soared. Next year, he was going to rent a hall so he could watch Cindy unwrap hers with careful precision so she didn't rip the paper, and Tony, who always skipped the card and went right for the prize.

"You are the best, Sullivan Forrest," said Samantha as she made her way back to him, a bit of blue tissue paper clinging to her heel.

He wiped the sweat from his brow, grabbing the closest discarded paper box to fan his face. "It was a good turnout this year."

He reached for the small box with Samantha's name on it that was snuggled right at the base of the tree. She'd been his best friend for longer than they had worked together, and he maybe cheated every year to make sure he always got her name.

"Oh dear, I wonder what that could be," she said with a fake gasp, taking the small package. "And who could it be from? I feel like they know my colors." She glanced from the bright pink paper to her matching shoes.

"Just open it." He fought down his flush as she opened the box, tugging the tissue paper out and tossing it to the side. It wasn't hard to match when that exact shade of pink was her favorite.

"Oh, Jesus, will you marry me?" She pulled out the candied apple that was coated with chocolate and caramel, clutching it to her chest. It was almost a pound of pure sugar and calories, but it was one of her favorite things in the world. "Is it okay if I don't share?"

Laughing, he nodded. *That's why I bought two.* The apples were expensive as hell, but also one of the most addictive things on the planet.

"Thank you so much, Sully." She pulled him in for a hug and he returned the squeeze, trying not to smoosh her tiny body.

People frequently told him that he was built like a bear, which made sense, since he *had* accidentally ripped the lid clean off an industrial garbage bin once. *It's a long story.* Sometimes he didn't exactly know his own strength.

"Okay, so don't freak out." She set her apple carefully on a nearby table before reaching into her purse and bringing out a small box. "I maybe ignored the ten-dollar limit, but you're my best friend, and I'll spoil you if I want to."

Wrapped with blue paper and a gold ribbon that she'd probably spent an hour trying to perfect, it was heavy when he took it...much heavier than he'd expected.

"You're killing me, Sully. Just open the damn box."

"I'm enjoying the moment," he said with a wistful smile. "I might ask you for the receipt in a second, but for now, I'm imagining that you got me something that I'll love." He laughed as she smacked him.

"You can be replaced, you know." She stuck out her bottom lip in a pout. "Last year's wasn't that bad."

"It was a bag of coal," said Sullivan, raising one brow. He hadn't been *that* bad.

"It was charcoal for the barbecue. All the guys were freaking out about this awesome charcoal that made their pork chops taste perfect." She rolled her eyes.

"I don't have a barbecue." He gave her a level stare, trying to keep his fond smile at bay. She was a great friend, but sometimes she was a bit scatterbrained.

"Okay, I made that part up. I forgot last year, and it was the only thing at the store that wasn't like fifty bucks. It was either that or waterproof matches." She let out a sigh. "They aren't always that bad."

He begged to differ. Two years ago he'd gotten an actual mousetrap. It had come in a box, and she'd claimed that she'd thought it was the board game.

Not to mention the expired coupon from the year before that.

Or the Starbucks gift card with a balance of four dollars and thirteen cents.

"I'm holding my breath over here," said Sullivan, looking at the box. It fit just in his palm, so he doubted that it was lethal—unless she'd wrapped him a jar of cyanide.

"I had a trusted friend give me solid advice on it this time, so if you don't like it, you can take it up with him." She tapped her foot impatiently.

"I'm your only friend."

His laugh died as he unwound the ribbon, ripping the paper and pulling the top of the box open. His breath caught, his eyes tearing up immediately. "It's…"

"It's your parents," she said, touching the necklace and turning the charm so it was the right way up. It was rectangular, similar to a military dog tag and was attached to a thick chain. Instead of a name and number, there was an engraved picture of his parents. The amount of detail was astonishing, the carved lines capturing the smile on his mother's lips and the patient gleam of his father's eyes.

"I know they aren't with us anymore, but I thought you would want them with you for Christmas. This is the best way I knew how to make that happen for you."

He cleared his throat, touching his fingertip to the surface of the picture. It shimmered in the lights from the Christmas tree, the silver lines capturing every detail they'd had in life. "It's beautiful."

Samantha knew better than most how hard the loss had hit him. Every Christmas had been laced with tradition for him, but this one was going to be so different without them—no Christmas Eve dinner or Eggs Benedict on Christmas morning, no unexpected gifts that he told them every year not to get and no quiet moments of Dad reading to them in front of the fire.

Sniffing, he wiped his cheeks with the back of his hand, turning away before Samantha could catch him. He waited until he had himself under control again before he spoke. "It's passable."

Her smile was infectious, dragging his grief away as she grabbed the necklace from him and secured it around his throat. It settled against his sternum, a surprisingly heavy weight that was full of remembrance.

"I was going to steal some of their ashes from your mantel and put them in a little necklace for you instead, but Lincoln said that would be too creepy. He suggested the engraving and even set me up with a little shop downtown." She patted him once on the back before she pulled away, leveling him with a look. "You like it, though? Really?"

Who is Lincoln? He spent nine hours a day with the woman, and he was certain there wasn't anyone by that name in the company. She'd never mentioned him before, either. She had a *lot* of boyfriends, though, not that he was judging. It was better than his zero.

"I love it," he said, squeezing her shoulder. "Thank you so much, Samantha."

She waved him off, picking at one of her manicured nails where a bit of sparkling red had peeled away.

"Don't thank me. Thank Lincoln. He's the brains of the operation."

Okay... "Who is he, exactly?" A boyfriend was most likely. Samantha had gone through three dates in the last week, had three guys on trial at the moment, along with two in a long-term poly relationship. He had no idea how she found time for all of them.

Sullivan didn't have the attention span that she did. When he fell in love, he wanted to fall so deep that he'd never even want to look at another man again. Pouring out his soul to another human being and having them cherish it was the only thing he really wanted. Unfortunately, that was hard to come by for a hopeless romantic like himself, especially with his *quirks*.

"Oh." She bit her lip, looking around before she lowered her voice. "He's my pen pal."

What? He'd had a pen pal in grade school, but he'd lost touch with them after the semester had ended. He honestly didn't even know it was a thing anymore. With every kind of social media, pen and paper were on their way out.

"You know...from the *program*," she said, lowering her voice even more.

"*Oh.*" He looked around, eyeing up Harry who was lingering by the tree. "AA has pen pals?" He covered his mouth in case Joyce was watching. She could read lips like a pro, and he did not want to start any more rumors.

Samantha nodded once, her lips pressed into a line. "Not always, but I found this program and his name was in the system, so I reached out. Anyway, yeah, Lincoln is my pen pal. He's a great guy, really. He rambles on for pages about this and that, and it's always so interesting. I swear he's the smartest guy I've met—or not met, because I've only ever written to him. You should write him and thank him, though. It would be good for you. I'm sure he wouldn't mind if I gave you his address. It's just a PO box."

He curved his lips up, his laughter nearly bursting through him. "Somebody has a crush."

He hadn't seen her so hung up on a guy since eleventh grade when Perry Larson had transferred to their high school and had taken the halls by storm.

"Shut up," she pushed his shoulder playfully, barely budging him. Her cheeks flushed.

"You know what? I *will* write to him." If nothing else, it would keep Sullivan's mind off his first Christmas alone.

Chapter Two

Fifteen days until Christmas

Dear Lincoln,

Sullivan paused with his hand hovering over the paper. He'd gone to Office Depot when he'd discovered that all he had were notepads and a few crumpled pages of lined sheets that were probably from his high school days.

Perhaps he'd gone a bit over the top with the watermarked red paper with green Christmas trees and small blank spots that were probably supposed to be snow—that, and the gold envelopes he'd found in the clearance section and the envelope stickers of little snow-covered cardinals.

He touched the charm at his neck, dragging his fingertip over the engraving. He could have spent a hundred dollars more, and it still would have been worth it. Every time he caught sight of the charm in the mirror, he was elated and grieved. He hadn't taken it off since Samantha had put it around his neck, either.

He'd started the letter three times, not quite sure what to say to a total stranger. It was hard to tell the truth and just lay it out, even without looking someone in the face.

Dear Lincoln,
I'm not sure how much Samantha has told you about me, but I'm her best friend, Sullivan. We just had our gift exchange at work and...

He bit the back of his pen, ink already soaking into his fingertips from a crack in the plastic. When was the last time he'd written a letter that wasn't for work?

She said that you picked out the gift for me. I don't know if you understand how perfect it is. I only lost my parents recently, and they were everything to me. Having them with me again for Christmas, even if it's just an engraving, means the world.
I wish I could do something for you in return. I don't know if you wanted to go for coffee, but the offer is there. Samantha said she's never met you, so maybe I'll just leave my address with you instead. If you ever need someone to talk to, I'm your guy.
So much more than a thank-you.
Sullivan Forrest

Sullivan let out a breath, setting the pen down as his hands began to shake. His apartment was empty, and even the warm glow of the tree's lights did nothing to quell the cold that seeped into his gut. The pictures on the walls looked bleak in the dim light of early morning, and the white landscape of fresh snow outside his window was especially miserable.

Loneliness fucking sucked, especially elbow deep in the holiday season.

There was one piece of solace that had come to him the night before when he'd still been on the fence about contacting Lincoln. If Lincoln was in a pen pal group with Samantha, then maybe he'd gone through the same type of thing. Maybe someone to write to would make his Christmas. Maybe it would stave off his loneliness if Lincoln was looking out into the snow from his own window in an empty apartment.

After folding the paper in three, he tucked it into the envelope, sealing it with a few of the cardinal stickers. It looked more like a kid's craft than the professional letters he was used to.

Only one problem left.

He usually had to mail his Christmas cards weeks or months ahead of the season for them to make it in time. It was only a few days until Christmas, and the postal service might not get it there before the big day. He *needed* to thank Lincoln right away so he would know how much his gift was appreciated.

Setting the envelope in the little bowl next to his front door, he pulled on his coat and boots, following up with a pair of mittens that he had sewn himself. Luckily, he'd inherited his mother's talent for sewing, and he had enough pairs to last a few ice ages. His favorites had cartoon reindeer on the knuckles. He'd found the fabric in the discount bin at the fabric store in the middle of July and hadn't let it go to waste.

It was just starting to snow as he stepped outside, the flakes floating on the breeze that was swirling between the buildings. A few cars honked in the Friday morning traffic, the main intersections thick with pedestrians.

Glancing at the letter for the third time, he turned down the main street before heading to the post office. The place would probably be packed, and he spotted an Amazon truck out front unloading what looked like fifty packages.

The cold had started to soak through his mittens by the time he stepped into the building, the bell chiming above the door as he entered. Off to the left was an area with a few hundred little boxes, each with a keyhole and a number on it. It was shiny and sleek, like the gateway to hundreds of lives.

A second bell chimed as he pushed through another door and stepped up to the counter. A tired-looked middle-aged man stood behind it, giving him a sweet smile as he approached.

"Can I help you?"

Row and rows of envelopes and boxes lined the wall, along with a few advertisements for coin collections. *Do people buy coins from the post office?* It seemed like a strange mix.

"Hi, um…hi." He cleared his throat, tearing his eyes away from the shiniest gold coin he'd ever seen. "I need to deliver a letter—*this* letter." He slid the envelope across the counter toward the clerk. "I wanted him to get it right away, so I was going to hand-deliver it, but it's just a PO box. I'm not sure how fast you can get it to him, but I'll pay extra if you can get it there today."

Even though he'd waffled with the idea of sending the letter in the beginning, he needed Lincoln to get it *now*. He couldn't go another day without thanking the man who had thought of the best Christmas gift in the world. Being a good influence for Samantha was just a happy side effect.

The worker gave him a small nod before grasping the letter and setting it on the little scale beside him. "It looks like it's just the standard weight and size, and that post office box is part of this office, so I could bend the rules a little for you and rush it through." He shot Sullivan a wink that warmed his gut.

"Don't worry. You aren't the only one with last-minute Christmas cards. I had a lady in here this morning with two hundred of the things." He shrugged, ringing up the till. "My husband and I usually send everything out in November or it's late, and I *work* here."

Sullivan chuckled and he let out a sigh of relief, a burden suddenly lifting from his shoulders.

"I'll be right with you, sir," said the clerk to someone over Sullivan's shoulder.

Sullivan looked back in surprise. He couldn't remember hearing the bell chime after he'd pulled the door shut.

His heart lodged in his throat as he took in blue eyes, dark hair streaked with a touch of gray and a strong jawline that was in the definition of 'silver fox'.

"Oh my." Sullivan slapped a hand over his mouth, flushing as he turned back to the counter and fished out his dollar and seven cents. The chuckle behind him had his hands shaking, his change falling to the soggy mat below his feet.

"Here. Let me, handsome," a voice said.

Sullivan backed up against the counter as the silver fox stooped with a grin, snatching the change off the ground before leaning close and passing the postal worker the money.

Gawking like a fish, Sullivan flushed hot as he caught a whiff of expensive cologne and leather. He could almost feel the warmth from their proximity alone. It wasn't often he saw someone who was exactly his type and wasn't a figment of his imagination, and *damn,* he was fine.

"Th-thanks." Sullivan snapped his mouth shut, afraid of what else he would say. *Ask him for his phone number. No, just ask him out for coffee. Speak up, idiot!*

"No problem." The silver fox winked. "You have a Merry Christmas and stay safe out there. Some freezing rain just started up, and it's getting pretty slick."

Slick. Oh goodness, didn't that bring on welcome thoughts.

Sullivan nodded numbly before he sidestepped and practically ran for the door. *Idiot!* He was in his thirties, for Christ's sakes, and he'd picked up his fair share of men—usually at bars, but that wasn't the point.

It's been a while. Even longer since someone had called him 'handsome'. Between his beard and his size, Sullivan was more burly than 'handsome'.

Almost two years before his parents had passed, his last boyfriend had dumped him for another man. He hadn't been overly heartbroken, although Samantha had been outraged on his behalf. Since then, between work and grief, he hadn't really felt like going to a bar or club to pick someone up.

The chime above the door clanged as he pushed it with too much force. When he looked back, the silver fox was already checking in with the clerk, handing over his identification as the worker gathered a stack of mail and boxes for him. He'd obviously already forgotten Sullivan.

But Sullivan wouldn't forget him anytime soon.

Chapter Three

Sullivan startled at the knock on his door, pausing the television and checking his phone. *No text. That's weird.* People didn't usually show up to his place unannounced unless it was his neighbor...in which case, it was probably best to hide. She hadn't run out of excuses to visit, and he'd given her almost every ingredient under the sun in her pointless quest to get him on a date.

Sighing, he tossed the television remote then jogged to the door as the knock came a second time. One part of the floor squeaked underfoot as he approached, and he nearly tripped over the festive mat he'd set in the front hall. At least it kept his feet from getting soaked by his sloppy boots every time he walked by.

The lock clicked open under his hand, and he tugged the door wide, a bit of cooler air sneaking inside. Someone must've left one of the hall windows open again.

"Um, hello?" Sullivan tilted his head at the man standing in the hall. He was dressed in a three-piece suit, with an open jacket over top that looked like it had rolled off the latest runway. His hair was styled to perfection, except for the few melting snowflakes clinging to his tresses and the single strand that had escaped the mold. Even his nails looked polished, with a silver envelope clutched between his delicate fingertips.

The man raised one brow before placing a hand on his hip and cocking it out to the side. *If looks could kill, I'd be in a coma, at least.*

"Are you Sullivan Forrest?"

"Yes?" Sullivan blinked as the man handed him the crisp silver envelope before turning on his heel and marching down the hall. "Um...Merry Christmas?" He looked at the letter in his hand and the neat printing of his name and address. There weren't many people who had penmanship that nice anymore. Even Sullivan's own writing was a messy scribble in comparison.

Pinching himself once, just to make sure he hadn't fallen asleep on the couch and was in the midst of a weird-ass dream, he headed back inside, staring down at the envelope. *What the hell?*

He peeled back the sticky seal, the glue still fresh and pliable. Inside was a single piece of paper that had been folded three times, diluted ink shining through the creased page. Carefully opening it, he flipped on the lamp, leaning close to read the pristine calligraphy.

Dear Sullivan,

I'm overjoyed that you liked your gift. I'm not going to lie to you. A Christmas alone is fucking terrible. I've been doing it for ten years, and I can list the things that don't make it better. Alcohol is on the 'no' list, even if it's in eggnog and you're trying to be festive and all that crap. Trying to completely ignore the big day doesn't work either, because somebody's Christmas cheer will rain on that parade...

Sorry. I'm rambling. I guess I assumed you would be alone, too, but I'm not sure if you're married and have three kids or whatnot. I try to steer clear of asking Samantha about relationships, if you know what I mean, so I don't know much about you. Tell that woman she can have ten men, and she'll find a way to make it twelve. But no judgment on my part, as long as she's happy.

What was I writing about? The intern keeps distracting me. Sorry. Someone needs to tell that guy that the 'bitch look' is not in style.

If you're alone – or even if you aren't – hit me up with another letter. I could use the company around the holidays. That, and checking in at the post office keeps me from watching all these tear-jerker movies. I swear, if I cry one more time during It's a Wonderful Life, *I'm checking myself back into rehab.*

What's your favorite Christmas movie?
Lincoln

Sullivan read the letter a second time, then a third. It really was a rambling mess, but also funny...in a sad sort of way.

He glanced outside to where the freezing rain was still pouring down and coating the sidewalks in a thick layer of glass. He'd gotten home before the worst of it, but the storm had strengthened in the last few hours. The time on his watch said it had only been three hours since he'd left the post office. He almost wanted to go back, even with the conditions outside.

Maybe the silver fox would still be there.

He may or may not have jerked off when he got home, his jacket still on and the faintest scent of cologne clinging to him. But that was between him and his half-empty bottle of lube.

His cuckoo clock peeped, the time displayed in antique Roman numerals. Three hours and Lincoln had somehow picked up the letter, written back and delivered a new one.

The guy in the hall? No. There was no way. The Lincoln he imagined was a touch taller and way less condescending and judgmental than that guy had been. He could picture him in a suit, though.

Tossing the letter on the table, Sullivan tried to crush the rising enthusiasm that was bubbling in his gut. It didn't make sense to get excited about someone he'd never met, but at the same time...

He grabbed a fresh piece of paper before he could decide to back out, digging out the same pen he'd used the last time so it would match. The ink level had gotten lower in the chamber, a small blue puddle stamped on the inside of the drawer. He dabbed the tip on a tissue before half-heartedly trying to clean up the mess.

Dear Lincoln,

I cry every time I watch that movie, if it makes you feel any better. But my favorite Christmas movie is probably The Godfather. *Samantha hates it, but she has no taste in movies, as you probably know.*

I had a thought...

He brought the pen to his mouth. His lips were probably stained blue, but he couldn't bring himself to care.

Could we ever talk on the phone? Letters are okay, but I would like to hear your voice and thank you properly.

He had to hold himself back from scratching the line out and starting over. He sounded so fucking desperate—and maybe he was. But he didn't want to come on too strong and scare off a potential new friend. He also didn't need anything to do with a relationship and wanted to make that clear.

I'm married, but my husband will be away over the holidays, as he always is...

That sounded about right—not too desperate because he was already married, but lonely all the same. *And apparently, I'm married now.* Maybe he would get some of the benefits too, like someone else doing his laundry. *Doubtful.*

Scribbling out a few more lines, he attached his phone number to the bottom. He folded the paper neatly, then slid it into an envelope and sealed it shut with a long sigh.

No going back. Samantha was going to kill him.

Chapter Four

Thirteen days until Christmas

"How can you watch that?" asked Sullivan as he slid the tray of little gingerbread men into the oven. Some of them had gone a touch flat, but the dough tasted fine to him. Once they had a pound of icing on them, they'd be fine either way.

Samantha turned to him from her perch on the couch, shooting him a glare. Grabbing the remote, she dialed up the volume, leaning back into the couch with an exaggerated sigh.

"I love this part, Sully." She clutched the closest pillow and hugged it to her chest. "She's just about to meet her prince charming and she doesn't even know it yet. Her life is so perfect, but just wait. It gets even better."

Of course, he knew. He'd liked the movie the first three times. The next hundred…not so much. If he had his guess, she'd probably watched it a dozen times since November first.

"I wish my hair looked that good rolling out of bed." She twisted her fingers through her hair, killing the look that she'd probably spent half an hour on. "Come on, though. If you look that perfect after bed, then you aren't doing it right." She tossed the pillow, crossing her arms.

"Um, she's alone?" Sullivan's mind dropped straight to the gutter. His hair wouldn't be the only totally fucked part of him if he went to bed *with* someone. He tried to be more reserved when he was alone, though.

Samantha shot him another glare with a single raised eyebrow. "You need to get laid."

Valid…but not happening.

"I can hear your cliché thoughts from here, my friend," she said, thankfully lowering the volume a touch before she strolled to the kitchen. "I hope you have better luck finding prince charming. I've struck out so many times lately that I don't even remember what a diamond looks like anymore."

He wrapped his arms around her, pulling her in for a quick hug. Just because he wasn't polyamorous himself didn't mean that he wasn't understanding of his friend. Of course, there was always a little teasing, but he got it back ten-fold. She was pretty insistent that she would never take her vows with a single man, though.

"And your phone has been vibrating for the last five minutes." She pointed at the table to where it was moving around as it buzzed away quietly. "You better pick up. It's probably work, or better yet, prince charming."

"Hardy-har-har." He rolled his eyes, even as his stomach flopped and he rushed for his phone. He'd sent his letter two days before, but he hadn't heard anything from Lincoln. He honestly hadn't expected to at this point. He'd bitten his lip raw wondering if he'd pushed too far, while feeling terrible for his lie at the same time.

The ID on the screen was blocked. *Probably spam.* Chewing his lip, he took a deep breath. "Hello?"

There was a long pause, and Sullivan looked back to his phone just to make sure it had actually connected. He could *hear* someone on the other end, with their small breaths and a murmur of distant conversation.

"*The Godfather* is *not* a Christmas movie."

Sullivan melted onto the couch as he muted the television, holding the phone tight to his ear. Lincoln's voice was everything he'd imagined and beyond. It was soft and deep, with a quiet rumble that just made him want to hug the man even more. *Totally platonically, because I'm apparently married.*

"Yes, it is," said Sullivan once he was able to speak again. He couldn't count the number of times he'd had this conversation with Samantha. Just because it didn't exactly have a Christmas *theme* didn't mean that it wasn't a Christmas movie.

"They're out buying presents when Michael's father is shot, and there's Christmas music playing in the background—ergo, Christmas movie." He smiled as Lincoln's chuckle answered him.

"Please tell me you don't have kids to go along with that husband, because they'll be scarred for life."

Sullivan snickered, leaning back and closing his eyes as his guilt disappeared. Lincoln sounded almost relieved about the fact that he was supposed to be married. "I'm glad you called."

He opened his eyes at the sound of Samantha tapping closer on the laminate flooring. He caught her eye, pressing his finger to his lips. She scrunched her face, tilting her head in question.

"I almost didn't," said Lincoln, letting out a sigh. "I wasn't sure what calling would mean, really. Pen and paper are my jam. Gets it all out of my head and gives it to someone else to read and keep, but this talking stuff...? I dunno."

Sullivan sat up, his heart dropping. "I'm so sorry. I didn't mean to make you uncomfortable. You can hang up now and we can forget this ever happened."

Sullivan wouldn't forget the sound of Lincoln's voice anytime soon. He'd been building a picture in his mind, and his voice was just one more puzzle piece. He needed to figure out the man who somehow *knew* him, even when they were strangers.

"Nah. Then I wouldn't be able to ask what your second favorite Christmas movie is."

Sullivan grinned, pointing from Samantha to the door. He was officially kicking her out of his apartment. She crossed her arms, tapping her foot impatiently while mouthing 'who is it?'.

"*Girl With the Dragon Tattoo.*"

"Oh, dear, sweet baby Jesus." Lincoln laughed. "That's not even... No, just no. You have to pick a different one, and it has to be Christmassy."

Sullivan jumped as the cookie timer started to chime. He darted for the kitchen, wincing at the thick scent of burnt ginger. "Oh crap, my cookies just burned. Just a second. I've got to set you down."

He tapped the speaker button, grabbing his oven mitts from the drawer before tugging the oven door open. A wall of smoke greeted him, rushing toward his face and stinging his eyes. "Ah, fuck, I'm blind."

"What the hell is going on?"

He caught Lincoln's shout over the sound of the timer, but just barely. Flicking the annoying buzzer off, along with the oven, he tugged the cookies out of the oven and dropped them straight into the sink, starting up the cold water.

The pan snapped and sizzled, the small embers on the one gingerbread's foot dying as it was soaked. Sullivan winced as a second round of steam billowed into his face. "Sorry... I burned my damn cookies."

He grabbed for the tap to shut the water off, but his wrist touched the edge of pan that hadn't cooled. Hissing, he drew back, a red line already forming. "And me... I burned me, too."

The fire alarm blared to life over his head, flashing and breaking his eardrums to pieces as it warned him to evacuate. He screamed over the noise, clutching his chest while running for one of the chairs at the island counter. He scrambled onto it, teetering as he swatted at the alarm. Finally finding the button, he plunged the apartment into silence.

His ears rang as he blinked the tears from his stinging eyes. The smoke was thick at the height of the ceiling, clogging his lungs until he choked for breath.

Stepping down, he hung his head, looking to the silent phone where the timer was still counting. Lincoln hadn't hung up, surprisingly. He must've thought Sullivan was an absolute lunatic, though.

"So, now that I'm deaf *and* lonely, what's your second favorite Christmas movie?" asked Lincoln.

Sullivan choked out a laugh, glancing over to Samantha, who was looking at him like he'd lost his mind. Wiping the tears from his eyes, he peered at his poor little cookies that would never be iced.

"*Star Trek Generations.*"

Lincoln made a vaguely inhuman squawk. "That's it, we're done. Get your popcorn ready because the next time I call you I'm going to have a *real* list for you to watch. See ya, Sullivan."

The line clicked as Lincoln hung up.

Sullivan stared at the phone, his heart still racing. He'd *spoken* to Lincoln, when even Samantha had never succeeded. The whole idea of it somehow seemed magical and like he was living in some kind of holiday dreamland.

"Who was that? You catch a guy that I don't know about?" Samantha crossed the kitchen, poking at the burned and soggy cookies. "You could probably salvage these. Icing fixes everything…even little houses."

His mouth went dry as he grabbed the cookies and tossed them into the trash before Samantha could attempt to 'salvage' them. *Should I say anything?* "Just a friend. Nothing more than that."

"Huh, too bad. He sounded hot."

Yes. Yes, he did. Maybe Sullivan would look a little mussed after rolling out of bed alone after all with a voice like *that* in his memory.

Grabbing the spatula, he scraped the stubborn bits into the trash, finding a second roll of dough that he'd prepared as a backup. It wasn't his first kitchen incident.

"Random question for you," he said, grabbing his rolling mat and pin. He tossed a bit of icing sugar on the mat because he hated how flour tasted on the surface of rolled cookies.

"Shoot." She drew her finger through the sugar, popping it into her mouth.

"That pen pal program you mentioned. Do they ever meet up in person or anything like that? I wasn't sure how it worked." He kept his gaze on the dough as he started to roll, his T-shirt straining as he pushed a bit too hard and his biceps bulged.

Too thin again. Dammit. Lincoln had him totally off his game. He wasn't sure if he had enough molasses for a third batch if this one went up in smoke.

"Nope." Samantha looked oblivious as she grabbed another fingerful of sugar. "It's kind of anonymous, just like the meetings. I wouldn't know Lincoln if I saw him on the street or anything, and I have enough shit on my plate to even think about texting him, even if I did have his number."

A strange warmth filled his belly. Was it a bad thing to feel special?

"Why? You looking to get a pen pal? I can give you the info about the program if you want."

Sullivan slowly shook his head as he grabbed the cutter and pressed out another dozen little men. "No, just wondering how it worked. I didn't know something like that could be therapeutic, but if it helps you, then I'm happy you found it."

She snagged the leg off one of the men before he could slide it onto a fresh baking sheet. He *accidentally* smooshed the rest of it, passing it to her without looking.

"Friends can be overrated sometimes," she said, talking around the dough in her mouth. She leaned against the counter, a bit of powdered sugar dropping from her clothes and spreading over the surface. "I love you, Sully, but you know me too well. You know what

I am at my best and worst, and you have *expectations* for me. Sometimes I just need to vent to a stranger and know that I'll never have to really talk to them again. Whatever I say, it won't come back to bite me somehow or ruin our relationship."

He rolled that one over in his head as he transferred the last cookie. He *did* have expectations for her, even if it wasn't deliberate.

"Don't think I don't know what you're trying to do," she said, poking his chest. "Tell me all about your new friend. I want details, including condom size. Does he treat you well?"

He choked on the piece of dough he'd stuck in his mouth, spitting it onto the floor near her foot by accident. It was as if she knew exactly what he'd been wondering.

"Ew, you spit on me." Pre-chewed dough and red nail polish did not match. "That's it. Your *friend* on the phone was right. You're impossible. I'm going to watch my movie some more. Call me when it's time to decorate these babies."

"Does he treat you well?"

He looked to his phone, wishing Lincoln's number had somehow saved and hadn't been blocked. The volume on the television cranked up again, and he let his eyes fall shut, picturing what Lincoln would do if he were in the kitchen beside him. "Yes."

Chapter Five

Seven days until Christmas

Sullivan glanced at his grocery list again, looking up the aisle for the boxed stuffing that had to be hiding somewhere. The shelves were nearly bare except for a few vegetarian options, and the store itself was packed beyond capacity.

He stepped back as two women fought over the last jar of cranberry sauce. Their husbands conversed amicably to the side as the crumpled can fell from one woman's hand, rolling under the shelf, probably never to be seen again.

Fresh cranberries, it is. He might have been planning the menu for a Christmas dinner for one, but he was still going all out. He'd picked out the nicest chicken in the store, and it would probably last him four meals.

Leaving the brawl behind, he headed for the fresh produce before he could forget. He had to squeeze his way past a family at the end where a toddler was pouring boxes of cookies into the cart unnoticed while his dad chatted with someone.

Everyone except him seemed to know somebody, which wasn't exactly true. He had Samantha and close to a hundred colleagues who he could talk to for hours, but his life outside of work was a touch dismal of late. He'd pulled away from a lot of people during his grief, and he hadn't made the time to reconnect.

Except with Lincoln.

As if summoned by some sort of higher being, Sullivan's phone buzzed in his coat pocket, vibrating against his hip uncomfortably. Setting down his bag of cranberries, he grabbed his phone, smiling at the display.

"Hey, Lincoln, what's the doom and gloom for today?" Sullivan grinned as he heard Lincoln's typical snort on the other end. They'd been talking every day, sometimes more than once, and Sullivan had finally started to peel back the layers of his mystery man.

He's just as lonely as I am.

"Where are you? It's too early for a nightclub," asked Lincoln.

Sullivan cupped his hand over his cell, wincing as a child screamed somewhere in the store. "Just out getting groceries for my super-depressing Christmas feast. I managed to get the last bag of cranberries because they were all out of cans."

"Please don't tell me that you're cooking them. You'll burn the house down!" Lincoln cackled as if it were fucking hilarious. Sullivan glared at the phone. A woman gave him the side-eye as he passed her, taking a step back.

"Not funny. I'm a good cook as long as I'm not distracted," said Sullivan, sending the lady an apologetic smile and tuning down his glare. Sometimes he forgot how intimidating people found him.

"Am I distracting you?" asked Lincoln.

Oh dear. Sullivan pushed his cart toward the teller, so ready to be done with the crowd. Every time Lincoln had called him, he'd managed to drop, smash, burn or break something. Even now, he was barely holding onto his cart, his grip all funky and his phone already slipping. His stomach was flipping, too, which was unreal, because he'd never even met Lincoln.

A few handfuls of conversations and he already felt like they were best friends—more than that, when he let his mind wander late at night. It had been doing a lot of that lately.

"You still there?"

"Yeah, sorry," said Sullivan. "Just paying for my groceries now, then I'll be on my way home. I'm on *Home Alone* number three, but I have to admit that I'm not really feeling it."

When Lincoln had called him with a list that was nearly one hundred movies long, Sullivan's hand had cramped trying to write them all down quickly enough. It had been a rough start, but *actual* Christmas movies—as Lincoln called them—were starting to grow on him.

"You can skip that one if you want. The first two are great, but it's all downhill from there. What's next up?"

Sullivan grabbed his bags, hefting them from the cart and heading for his car. His receipt caught in the wind as soon as he opened the door, the small piece of paper fluttering off into the parking lot.

"I dunno," he said. "Some guy made me this massive list that I have no way of finishing in time. I didn't exactly memorize it." *Total lies.* Next was *Christmas Vacation*, then *White Christmas*. He'd studied that list as if he were obsessed, which he kind of was, if he had to admit it.

"A few all-nighters and it will be over," said Lincoln. "Get that husband of yours to keep you up. Shouldn't be that hard."

Sully's stomach dropped. The lie still felt terrible, even if he'd had the best intentions. That, and his fake husband was starting to cramp his style.

"He's out of town already." He tried to dredge up some non-existent grief from being left alone. It wasn't hard to pretend.

"Then what about Samantha? She can't be that busy with all her boys."

He started the car, switching the call to Bluetooth. "She has two family parties on her side, and I think three on the other sides, so far."

"Well fuck." Lincoln paused for a moment. "Hell, why not? Would your man have an issue if we made it a night together? I'll bring the root beer and popcorn and keep you awake all night, and you make me dinner in exchange. I hope you have a comfy couch, though."

Oh dear. Am I dreaming? Sullivan pinched his arm, just to be certain. It hurt like hell, even through his coat. "Sure. I don't think he'll have an issue with it. I've told him all about you." There were so many imaginary conversations to try to keep track of.

"I'll see you in ten." The line went dead.

Ten? Ten! If he put the pedal to the metal, then he might make it back to his apartment in seven minutes, but with holiday traffic and a full load of groceries, there was no way he would make it in time.

Not to mention that he hadn't exactly cleaned after his last round of baking. There was still flour all over the counters and a heaping garbage bag full of pastry dough. And he was presentable for the grocery store, but not a first meeting or date...

This is not a date. This is the furthest thing from a date.

He glided into his parking spot eleven minutes later, grabbing his bags and rushing to the front door of his apartment. He fumbled for his keys, his bags slipping and nearly pitching onto the ground.

"Need a hand?"

Sullivan whirled, one bag slithering from his hand and tumbling to the icy path. Breaking free, his cranberries smacked straight into the pile of slush at his feet. His breath caught, his face burning as he caught sight of the man walking up the path behind him.

It was the second time he'd snuck up on Sullivan, and he definitely didn't belong in the building. A silver fox like him, with rugged looks and the bluest eyes he'd ever seen, should have been in a high-rise penthouse, not in a post office or a shitty apartment building.

"You don't live here," said Sullivan, because apparently, he'd gone brain dead when he'd lost his cranberries. Sullivan flushed hotter as the man chuckled.

"Sure don't. I'm visiting a friend...unless there's a toll." He winked.

"Oh, Christ no. Sorry. You just um...startled me, that's all." Setting his bags on a dry spot on the ground, Sullivan reached for the cranberries, brushing what slush he could off the package.

"You must startle easily. It's not the first time I've caught you daydreaming."

He remembers me? Sullivan blinked, his mouth going dry. *Please tell me that he can't read my mind.* It wasn't often that he remembered a man clearly enough that he could star in a few late-night fantasies. That was all

Sullivan could see now, staring at the stranger's jacket and picturing what lay underneath.

"There he goes again," said the silver fox, shaking his head and looking to where Sullivan's hand was frozen midway through cleaning off the cranberries. "I'll take it as a compliment, and please accept my humblest apologies for distracting you. I can still give you a hand, though. In a completely platonic way...or not."

"I'm...uh." This guy couldn't be for real. He looked serious, despite the laughter in his eyes, but Sullivan had been fooled before. There was no menace, though. Sullivan wasn't terrible-looking himself, but no one ever propositioned him quite so...directly.

"You have to buy me a drink first?" Sullivan said slowly, his mind still dragging as he stared at the guy's lips. They looked soft and perfect, with just a hint of scruff that would scratch him just right—as long as he didn't mind Sullivan's beard. Some guys weren't into it.

The man chewed his lip, looking between Sullivan and the door as if he were seriously considering it.

"I can't believe I said that. I'm so sorry. You already said you were meeting your friend and I'll...I'll open the door for you." Stuffing the damn cranberries in his bag, Sullivan twisted the key in the lock and tugged it open, waving the man past him. "Have fun with your friend." Sullivan rushed to get the words out, holding the door like a gentleman, even though the other bag was starting to slip.

"Have fun with your hand." The man winked, slipping along the hall and up the stairs.

Sullivan's bags hit the floor as he gaped, touching his face as he burned hotter. His eggs had probably smashed, but he couldn't bring himself to care. Oh, to have that kind of confidence. Sometimes it was a turn-off, but in this case it was bang on.

Next time. Next time he'd be on point and ask for the guy's name and number. At the very least, he'd be able to blow off some steam that was starting to reach boiling point.

Scooping up his groceries, he paused as his phone vibrated against his hip.

Where you at?

He let out a sigh as his breath caught for the second time in so many minutes. How could he be thinking about 'post office guy' when his very own real friend was waiting for him? He shot a quick *'almost home'* before he took off up the stairs, taking them two at a time as he clutched his groceries tight.

He stepped out of the stairwell, his heart stopping.

Leaning against his door with his phone in hand, looking like sex, sin and every dream Sullivan had ever had, was the silver fox.

I'm so screwed.

Chapter Six

"Sullivan?" Lincoln's mouth dropped open as Sullivan stepped up to his door, setting his groceries on the ground.

His hands trembled as he fetched his key, his tongue so tied that he wasn't sure if he'd ever be able to speak again. Lincoln was staring at him, those blue eyes laser-focused and seeing straight through his pitiful silence.

"S-sorry I'm late. Traffic was crazy," said Sullivan, keeping his gaze firmly focused on his door as he jammed the key in the lock. He bit his lip as Lincoln stepped to the side to give him enough room to open the door. Lincoln's cologne was thick in the air, Sullivan's every muscle going taut at the alluring scent.

"Well, fuck." Lincoln stepped back, rubbing his hand over his face as he chuckled. "Your husband would probably kill me if he found out that I just offered you a handy. In my defense, I didn't know it was you. I just thought you were an extremely attractive stranger."

The key slipped from Sullivan's fingers, and he cursed as it clinked on the ground. *Extremely attractive stranger?* He was never going to survive.

Lincoln's hand on his wrist stopped him, his lips pressed into a serious line for the first time. "Did I overstep? I can leave if I made you uncomfortable."

Shaking his head, Sullivan leaned into the touch unconsciously. Lincoln was warm, the contact sending a shiver up his arm. Sure, he was uncomfortable, but probably not in the way Lincoln thought.

"It's nice to meet you...again. For the third time...whatever." Grabbing his key, Sullivan twisted the knob, letting himself inside. "Please come in."

Lincoln cleared his throat, dropping his hand before slowly stepping inside. He gave the apartment a single look, which was about all it warranted. It was small, but cozy, every bit of decoration picked by himself or Samantha. There were a few bits of sewing he had around, but most of his work was stuffed into his closet in the bedroom.

I'm taller than him. It wasn't unusual, per se, but he'd imagine Lincoln to be taller—tall enough to pick him up and toss him around. He looked like he was in good shape, but Sullivan was solid and built for a life of lumberjacking.

"It's a nice place." Lincoln pulled his jacket off, hanging it on the hook, and Sullivan caught sight of the tag. *Burberry, holy shit.* There was probably more than a grand hanging off the jacket hook that he'd picked up at the hardware store for fifty cents.

Lincoln paused before a picture frame that was just inside the living room. He smiled, his eyes lighting up. "Your folks?"

Sullivan nodded, dropping his groceries in the kitchen before coming up behind him. Touching the medallion at his neck, he stared at the picture. His mom had started to lose weight in that photograph, and his dad's frame was far from what it had been in his youth. They had both been happy, which was worth more than anything.

"I'm sorry for your loss." Lincoln touched his shoulder, the heat of it searing straight through Sullivan's jacket that he'd forgotten to take off. "I was never close with my parents—hell I barely even talked to them—but I know what it's like to miss someone so much that you'd rather kick the bucket than go another day without them."

Reaching for the medallion, Lincoln pulled it out from Sullivan's hand, tugging his coat zipper down by a few teeth so he could presumably see it better. Every inch of Sullivan went tight, his heart thudding as he sucked in a breath.

"It turned out well." Lincoln flipped it over, leaning close enough that Sullivan could feel his breath against his neck. He shivered, sweat beading beneath his coat. It had been *way* too long.

"I have to put away the—uh—milk."

Sullivan took a step back, not sure if he'd even bought milk or not. Lincoln sent him a smile, seemingly unaffected by their proximity. "You want me to go?"

It had been so much easier on the phone. Even with his distraction, Sullivan had never lost the ability to speak. It probably had something to do with the intensity of Lincoln's gaze, or the starring role that he'd unknowingly taken in Sullivan's dreams.

"Please don't," he whispered, pulling his coat from his shoulders and tossing it toward the door. It landed in a pile next to the boot tray, slush probably soaking right into the fabric.

"I'm sorry. I was just really nervous about meeting you, and now you're here and I'm...rambling."

Lincoln shrugged. "You rambled on the phone, too, if it makes you feel any better. And there's nothing to be worried about. It's just little old alcoholic me."

Sullivan rolled his eyes, his nervousness finally starting to clear. "Recovering alcoholic, right? Three years sober is an accomplishment to be proud of." He turned to the kitchen, jamming things in place. *Bread goes in the silverware drawer, right?* A quick wipe of the counters and most of the flour was cleaned up, too.

Lincoln made a face. "You sound like my sponsor."

"Excellent. Seems like you've got a good one, then."

Lincoln waved him off. "Enough about me. You listen to me all the time." He looked around, pointing to the shelf where Sullivan's beta fish slowly floated to the surface of his tank. "Show me around, and show me a picture of this husband of yours before we crash on your couch."

Sullivan's stomach twisted. Maybe now was the exact right time to tell Lincoln that he'd fibbed a bit.

"You know what?" Lincoln plowed on, pausing by Sullivan's collection of videos that he kept around despite his multiple subscription services. "Cancel that. Is this your fucking Christmas collection? Please say no. I won't make it through the night if you think the *Alien* trilogy are Christmas movies."

Snorting, Sullivan strolled over to the tower, kneeling before plucking his favorite movies of all time out of the stack. "I save those ones for when I need a laugh. And these." He pointed to a few that had Lincoln looking like he was about to weep.

"Do you have any normal-people movies?"

"What? Like action movies? I've got a whole stack of those here, and the entire Marvel collection for when I'm in the mood to watch some great...acting." He paused, staring up from where he had kneeled and reaching for another movie without looking.

Lincoln towered over him, every inch the authority in the room. He was at the perfect height, Sullivan's lips only a few inches and layers away from a prize. Sullivan wanted to whimper and palm his cock at the same time. He cleared his throat instead.

"You can say they have great asses, you know. Every single one of them, male and female. I've never seen so many great asses in my life," said Lincoln, reaching for the package in Sullivan's hand and bringing it closer to his face, scrunching to read the fine print.

"This is some amazing ass." His cheeks tinted as he stared at the case.

What? Sullivan did a double-take at the Blu-ray, his blood going hot when he saw what he'd accidentally grabbed. His porn...his fucking favorite porn he owned.

So, maybe he had a bit of a Daddy kink, and that was completely obvious from the title. *Oh hell.*

He grabbed the Blu-ray, ripping it from Lincoln's hand and nearly dropping it twice in the scramble to get it back in the tower. It jammed sideways, sticking out enough so the back pictures were still visible. One was from his favorite scene where the bottom was holding himself open while his Daddy rimmed him.

He yanked it from the tower, lunging toward the couch. Shoving it underneath, he tucked it as far away from sight as possible.

"I would be willing to rearrange the list for something more like that," said Lincoln, recovering with inexplicable grace. "But only if one of them wears a festive hat, at the very least. I'd say an ugly sweater would do, but I don't want to cover up those chests. I'm a nipple man."

This is where I die.

Lincoln looked straight at him, his eyes going dark as he finally seemed to realize their position. He moved his hand until he was so close to touching Sullivan that Sullivan could feel the warmth of him. "Is your husband a nipple man?"

Sullivan swallowed and shook his head, accidentally brushing against Lincoln's palm. He didn't pull away, but it took everything in him not to lean into the touch. His piercing throbbed against his shirt.

"Good to know." Lincoln cleared his throat before stepping back and making his way toward the couch. He sat down with an exaggerated sigh, subtly adjusting himself.

Sullivan looked down. His cock was very obviously hard, tenting the front of his pants in an invitation. He turned slightly away so Lincoln hopefully wouldn't see. He didn't want to do anything until Lincoln knew that he wasn't actually married, and at the moment, he was at a loss for words.

"So I think we should jump straight to *White Christmas*, then break for dinner. There's a Thai place in town that I've wanted to try for a bit, and they deliver. My treat," said Lincoln as if nothing had happened — as if Sullivan wasn't harder than he'd been in months, if not longer.

"Okay." His voice came out raspy and deep, and Lincoln's gaze was back on him instantly, his eyes narrow.

"Come on up here, big boy. I won't overstep. I'm all talk but rarely play. Your virtue is safe with me." Lincoln patted the couch cushion. "That, and I don't know how big this guy of yours is, and I'd rather not end up in the hospital."

Chapter Seven

The first few minutes of the movie were filled with such terribly thick silence that Sullivan wondered if he *should* kick Lincoln out of his apartment. Maybe it had been better when they were near strangers with nothing more than words and feelings between them. Samantha was right. Letters were easier.

Lincoln shifted next to him, crossing his arms and leaning against the end of the couch. It wasn't exactly the most comfortable setup, because the couch didn't recline, but he had a small ottoman that he usually used for when he decided to binge-watch a new series.

He shuffled the fabric stool over, nudging it against Lincoln's feet. Lincoln shot him a bright smile, some of the tension easing from his shoulders.

"Thanks."

Sullivan melted, grabbing the throw next to him and tossing it on Lincoln next when he noticed the goosebumps on his bare arms. Seeing Lincoln all wrapped up in *his* things eased the last bit of uncertainty from his bones. *Now is my chance.*

"How was work?" Sullivan asked, ready to face-palm when he lost his courage at the last moment.

Lincoln made a face, tugging the throw tighter until he was tucked from chin to toes. "Busy. Shitty. People are stupid."

Sullivan snorted, moving from the couch to grab them the coffee that he'd set to brew when he'd put the groceries away. "You need a more positive outlook on things. People are great, just selectively and for a short duration. I love people." He could get along with almost anyone if they gave him the chance.

"You've never owned your own company," said Lincoln, shifting until he was deeper into the blanket with only his head exposed.

"True. I'm just a COO," he said with zero sarcasm. As the Chief Operations Officer, Sullivan still had people above him in the company to ask for advice. He wasn't sure what he would do if he didn't have someone like Samantha to turn to when things got rough. "People are afraid to talk to me sometimes because I'm a big guy and I don't look the friendliest. The beard probably doesn't help." He touched it thoughtfully. "But I could spend my entire day with someone and listen to their concerns and ideas, doing my best to understand where they are coming from."

"You want a job?" Lincoln grumbled.

"Nope." Sullivan leaned on the arm of the couch, tilting so he could bring his feet up on the cushions. "I like where I'm at. Everybody knows me, and I have a lot of friends there. How many employees do you have?"

"Enough to be driven to alcoholism," said Lincoln with another grimace. "Sorry, I shouldn't say that. To be honest, I don't know the exact number. Lots."

"You should talk to them more. You're probably busy making the executive decisions, but they're the ones on the floor, so to speak. Sometimes they can come up with a better way to do things than a team of engineers, and they'll save you a lot of money, too." Sullivan's stomach grumbled as he flicked the subtitles on the movie so he could follow it a bit better.

"That's it, you're hired. You start on Monday. You okay with a quarter mil to start? I can do more if you want." Lincoln shot his arm out of the blanket, pointing at the screen. "I love this part. Look at that dress!"

Sullivan chuckled, resting his head against the couch. A quarter-million dollars would be fantastic. He could buy a fancier fish than a beta, and maybe upgrade a few appliances in his apartment—not to mention a new sewing machine. The housing market was tough, but maybe he could find a place outside the city.

It was too bad Lincoln was joking.

The movie was almost over when Lincoln ordered their food, somehow offering a big enough tip that it was there in fifteen minutes. They divided the containers out onto plates, heading back to the couch to line up the next movie. Instead of the end seat, Lincoln slid into the middle, gathering a dozen or so of the decorative pillows from around the house and jamming them beside him.

He leaned back into the pillows, letting out a soft sigh as he cradled his plate in his hands. "My first order as your new boss is getting you a new couch with actual lumbar support. I don't know how you stand it."

Sullivan set his plate on the ground, standing and pointing at the small indents where he'd just been resting. "Those are *my* ass-grooves. It has taken me years to perfect them, which is why no one else is allowed to sit here...not even Samantha. I am *never* replacing this couch."

Lincoln shot him a smile. "You *do* have a spine. Here I was thinking you were just a pushover."

Tossing a new movie in, Sullivan grabbed his food, taking his seat again. "I'm a bit of a pushover." That was probably why people loved him. He inevitably gave in. He was surprised that he hadn't given in to Lincoln's persistent flirting all afternoon.

But Lincoln had kept his word. All talk and no play. *Unfortunately.*

With his belly filled to the brim with something that didn't burn his tastebuds off, despite his worries, his sleepiness surged.

"Are you still cold?" Sullivan asked, turning to glare at the thermostat that was much too far away. He kept his place chilly, but the cold never really bothered him. Lincoln was still buried under the throw on his nest of pillows, though.

Lincoln nodded, biting his lip as he looked away from the movie. "I didn't want to bug you about it, but yeah."

"Wait." Lincoln grabbed him as he went to stand. "I could just move closer? If you don't mind. It looks like electric heat in this place, and I know how expensive that can run."

Sullivan swallowed. They'd just gotten back into friend instead of flirt territory, and he didn't want to push it. His afternoon had been one of the most enjoyable in recent memory and so much more satisfying than a hookup. As long as he stayed married, it wouldn't evolve into one.

"Yeah, sure. I can still turn it up if you'd rather. I don't know how comfy I am."

"Switch places with me," said Lincoln as he stood, wrapping the throw around his shoulders as he moved. He wasn't a small guy, but he still managed to look like a toddler bundled up for a playdate in the snow.

Sullivan scooted over, leaning against the pillows until he was reclined almost comfortably. He grabbed a few more, shoving them under his lower back. "Ah no, my ass-grooves."

"Oh shush and warm me up." Lincoln took his spot, settling closer until he was half-lying on Sullivan, his head resting against his shoulder.

This is such a bad idea. He was hard instantly. Lincoln's hand touched his belly as he relaxed, the brush of his fingers against Sullivan's T-shirt like a live wire. He sucked in a breath, flinching from the touch as it went lower, settling just above his belly button.

Lincoln may have been a self-declared nipple man, but Sullivan was all about belly buttons. He could fuck one with his tongue for hours if he was given a chance. His own was so sensitive that he could come if he was tickled in just the right way.

"You okay?"

"Yeah. Your hands are cold." Sullivan breathed through the lie. They weren't cold at all. Every inch of Lincoln was burning hot, even his breath that tickled his throat.

"I can move if you're uncomfortable."

Sullivan looped an arm around Lincoln's shoulders before he could stop himself, pulling him tighter to his chest. He turned slightly, so Lincoln's head was on his pec instead of his shoulders. He was twisted uncomfortably with his feet still on the ground, but it was an easy discomfort to ignore.

"Your husband is going to be pissed if he sees us like this," whispered Lincoln, making a half-hearted attempt to pull back. "I shouldn't... We shouldn't."

Sullivan couldn't let go. Running a hand down Lincoln's back, he tried to soothe the tension in every muscle. "It's okay. He won't see."

Lincoln let out a humorless laugh, even as he melted. "That doesn't make it okay. I mean, I shouldn't even be here. I came on a whim because I couldn't fathom not knowing what you looked like for another day. And here I knew all along."

"Do you want to go?" asked Sullivan, holding his breath as Lincoln's cologne clogged every brain cell. Lincoln shook his head, burrowing deeper. "Then trust me. I've never been unfaithful in my life."

"Okay. Don't let me change that."

The movie flashed before them, but Sullivan hardly saw any of it. Every time he started to watch, Lincoln would shift. Sometimes it was to scratch an itch above his eyebrow or to reach over Sullivan for his cup of coffee that must've been cold long ago. He'd meet Sullivan's gaze, giving him a smile before he settled back and turned to the screen again.

Only Sullivan didn't look away. He watched the steady rise and fall of the blanket with each of their combined breaths and the way Lincoln would smile or grimace at what was happening on the screen.

He didn't dare move, not even when his own mouth went dry or when his bladder started to pang. No. If he moved, it would end, and he would wake up alone and friendless.

"You want to do one more?"

Sullivan blinked as Lincoln's gaze caught him off guard. The credits were rolling on-screen as white streaks across black. He nodded, unable to say a thing. When Lincoln moved, he had to struggle to keep from pulling him close again. Instead of complaining, he took the opportunity to relieve himself and refresh their drinks and snacks.

When he settled onto the couch, he left his feet up with space between his legs for Lincoln to settle between. When Lincoln returned from the bathroom with his face flushed, he settled right between his thighs without question, resting his back against Sullivan's chest and pulling the bowl of pretzels into his lap.

He fit perfectly and was just the right height for Sullivan to reach around and grab a pretzel from the bowl. There was no doubt that he was older than Sullivan...maybe even by ten years or more. His hair was streaked with a touch of gray that flickered every time the television brightened. The laugh lines around his eyes were just a tad deeper, too, along with the dark shadows under them.

"You tired?" Sullivan reached for another pretzel, resting his hand against Lincoln's side instead of bringing it back to his mouth. He left it there for as long as he dared before slowly pulling it away, chomping on the pretzel and reaching for the next.

On cue, Lincoln let out a small yawn, going tight against Sullivan as he stretched. "I don't usually sleep well. Best case scenario, I get a few hours between midnight and four."

"And worst case?" He moved his hand over Lincoln's belly this time, resting against the slight softness there. He was so warm and content that

Sullivan was almost certain that everything was a dream. If that were the case, he never wanted to wake up.

"I don't sleep at all...sometimes for days." Lincoln turned his head, resting his cheek on Sullivan's chest.

Can you hear my heart racing? That's for you. He was hard, too, but he wasn't sure how long he had been. Every time Lincoln shifted, he rubbed against him, and Sullivan had to bite back a moan. Lincoln had to feel it. He had to *know*.

"I couldn't imagine that." Dropping the pretzel, Sullivan tucked his finger under the hem of Lincoln's shirt. It had ridden up in the last half-hour, a tiny strip of bare skin visible with a dappling of hair down the middle.

Suppressing a shiver at the first touch of bare skin, Sullivan scraped back and forth ever so slowly. Lincoln closed his eyes, letting out a soft sigh. His skin was so soft, with that extra bit of padding that made him perfect.

"I could sleep right now. I don't think I've ever been so comfortable," said Lincoln, wriggling even closer somehow. He pushed his ass against Sullivan's cock, the throbbing hardness like steel between them. "Usually I hate sleeping next to someone, which is why I'm a big fan of casual hookups. Everything frustrates me—the way they breathe or snore, or every time they grab the blankets and mess up my warm bubble. But you're just a big comfy bear. I would stay here for days if you'd let me."

Sullivan was torn between the 'casual hookups' comment and the 'staying for days' one. He bit his lip to stop his intended confession. As far as he was concerned, he'd been married way too long anyway.

But he also didn't want to become a casual hookup in the next thirty seconds.

Something about Lincoln had sunk its teeth into him, and he didn't want to pull away any time soon.

"You can stay as long as you'd like." He tucked a second finger under Lincoln's shirt, pushing the boundaries as far as he dared. He was so warm and soft, even his hair, which should have been coarse and thick, was like goose down.

Lincoln snorted, rolling onto his side. His hip jammed straight into Sullivan's groin, taking his breath. Pre-cum slicked the inside his boxers. He was probably drenched, the sticky feeling not just from the sweat gathering between them.

"You won't say that when I get a craving and dump all your booze down the sink, or if I eat too much chocolate and puke all over your bathroom. I'm allergic to chocolate, by the way…but there's no way I'm *not* going to eat chocolate." His breath puffed against Sullivan's neck with every word, making his skin prickle.

"I'll hide the wafers I was going to do chocolate pretzels with." He motioned at the pretzels, which were about half an inch from falling off the couch. "I usually end up eating them all before, anyway, so no harm there. And as for alcohol, I only keep a bottle of wine or two around for cooking. You'll have to be content with dumping ten-dollar wine."

He grabbed the pretzels, moving them to the floor before they could tip on their own. Lincoln turned once they were gone, burying his face in Sullivan's chest.

"You disgust me," said Lincoln with no heat in his voice. "Never drink wine that's under one hundred dollars a bottle. You never know where the cheap shit has been. I won't have to worry about dumping it, though. Hopefully you don't have any Coke around the place?"

"Uh...no?" Sullivan slipped his hands over Lincoln's back, clutching him tight. "Wait. Are we talking soda or hard drugs?" He didn't have either. He did have a little weed stash, but that shit was legal, so he wasn't going to take any flack for it. He wasn't going to offer it to a recovering alcoholic without a chat first, though.

"S-soda," said Lincoln, dragging the word out like he didn't recognize it.

"Then no." He looked at the screen, blinking when he noticed the movie was half-over already.

"Drugs?" Lincoln sounded almost desolately hopeful this time, and Sullivan couldn't help but give him an extra squeeze.

"Not for you. Your pen pal is my best friend, remember? She mentioned that you guys have a few things in common." He couldn't imagine going through the same thing Samantha had, but he'd never turn away from her friendship, even if it hurt sometimes.

"Damn, I forgot you knew me. Here I just thought we were snuggly strangers." He hugged Sullivan back, his grip a lot stronger than it looked. "Just don't let me fall asleep. I want to see your reactions to the next film. It's a fucking classic."

"Okay." Sullivan dragged his fingers up Lincoln's spine, watching as he closed his eyes again, this time keeping them closed. Lincoln parted his lips as he let out a yawn, his breaths slowly evening out.

When Sullivan was certain that he was asleep, he reached for the remote that was tucked under the edge of the pillows, flicking the television off. He tugged the throw over them, placing it around Lincoln's sides and peering down to make sure his toes were covered.

He gave himself three seconds to let his mind wander. He imagined cupping Lincoln's ass once and giving it a tiny squeeze before he retreated back to his waist. Relaxing against the pillows, he closed his eyes, drifting off to sleep in moments.

Chapter Eight

Six days until Christmas

Sullivan woke up slowly. Warmer than he'd ever been during the winter, his back and shoulders ached as if he hadn't moved all night. Someone shifted on his chest, dragging against his erection, which probably explained some of his vivid dreams.

Lincoln.

Out of the dozen or so guys that Sullivan had dated, no one had ever made him feel the way Lincoln did. There was a nervousness in his limbs that he rarely experienced, and it circled his chest, adding to his fear of losing his new friend.

He couldn't remember the last time he'd snuggled with someone without expectations. Once a man found out about his submissive side, every back rub led to more, even if all he wanted was to be touched and cherished. Despite Lincoln's teasing and flirting, Sullivan had never felt safer and more at ease. There was no pressure for anything, no matter how much he was starting to crave it.

Sullivan stilled as Lincoln suddenly shifted and let out a yawning grunt. He kept his eyes shut and his breaths even with the worry that Lincoln wouldn't feel nearly as comfortable about the situation as he did.

"Fuck, boy." Lincoln's rumbling voice jolted through him as he pulled away from his chest. He was still for a long moment, but Sullivan could feel his gaze. "If only you were mine," Lincoln whispered, scraping a finger over Sullivan's lower lip. "I would treat you right and buy you anything in the world you'd ever need. I'd never leave you wanting. If only you needed a Daddy to look after you."

Sullivan struggled to stay still as the pressure against his lip increased. It felt like Lincoln's finger, but he wasn't sure. He wished it weren't. He wished he had the courage to open his eyes and suck whatever it was right into his mouth.

"Fuck, you're beautiful." Lincoln's voice was even lower as he shifted away, his touch disappearing.

Sullivan couldn't stand it any longer. It was almost as if he were intruding on a private moment he wasn't meant to hear. Lincoln was breaking his heart, and it was even worse because of his lie.

Letting out a groan, Sullivan stretched, blinking his eyes open as Lincoln stood from the couch. Lincoln was stretching by the time his vision cleared, the strip of skin visible along his belly drawing Sullivan in like a black hole.

"Fuck, what time is it?" Sullivan blinked at the light coming through the window that was much brighter than he'd imagined. The last number he'd seen roll across the clock had been ten in the evening. His teeth were gummy, his stomach insisting that it was late.

Lincoln paused as he glanced at his watch, his face going momentarily blank. "Eleven in the morning?" He blinked, striding over to the curtain and pulling it wide so sunlight streamed into the room, even brighter as it reflected off the thousands of snowflakes on the neighboring buildings.

Sullivan grunted, turning his face into the cushion to hide his burning eyes. He whirled back at the startling noise Lincoln made.

Lincoln's watch glistened as he looked from it to the landscape outside, furrowing his forehead with each glance. His frown deepened as he tapped his watch. It had to have been a Rolex or some equivalent, the jewels on the face nearly blinding in the sunlight.

"What's wrong?" Sullivan rolled from the couch, stretching until his back and shoulders cracked a few dozen times. "I hope you aren't pissed that I didn't keep you up last night. I couldn't stay awake, either."

"No, that's not..." Lincoln trailed off, grabbing the edge of the curtains and pulling them even wider. Sullivan had made the curtains himself, but the seams could only take so much tugging. "Is it *actually* eleven? My watch is broken, right? And there must be a bright-ass lamp outside or something."

The small cuckoo clock Sullivan had in the den chose that moment to chime. It had been silent in the darkness, its light sensor telling it to sleep in the dark. He strolled to it, checking the Roman numeral display.

"Technically, it was still ten when you asked, but now it's eleven. I don't think I've slept that late in a long time." If he made it to eight on weekends, he considered himself lucky, although eleven was pushing it into laziness territory. "I'll make you some breakfast."

He headed for the kitchen, glancing back when Lincoln didn't move, still glaring through the window. He whirled suddenly, marching to the kitchen and pointing a finger straight at Sullivan's chest.

"Did you fucking drug me?"

Sullivan froze with the coffee pot in hand and the water running in the sink. *Is this a joke?* "Are we talking Coke and coke again?" He tried to smile, but Lincoln only scowled.

"This isn't a fucking joke," Lincoln grumbled, poking Sullivan in the chest with one perfect finger. "I *never* sleep this late. Fuck, I never even *sleep.* Who put you up to this? Was it Debra? I told her to stay the fuck out of my life, but if she gave you some sleeping pills to slip me, I've fucking had it. I don't care what dirt she has on me. She's fucking fired."

"Um." Sullivan reached for the tap, awkwardly turning it off and setting the pot on the stove before he dropped it. "I shouldn't have joked, but I didn't drug you, and I have no idea who Debra is."

Lincoln shoved a hand down the back of his pants, screwing his face up in concentration. "I'm not sore, so I know we didn't do anything."

What? Sullivan's heart dropped to the level of his socks and the excitement that had been bubbling from the night before, popped into oblivion. "You aren't *sore*? Is that— Is that the kind of guy you think I am?"

Sullivan shook his head, blinking back the tears that suddenly threatened. In all his life he'd never been so insulted, humiliated or fucking shattered. His lips refused to move, and his throat shut tight as a sob tried to escape.

"Sullivan." Lincoln stumbled, his eyes wide as he suddenly seemed to realize what he'd implied.

"I'm not." Sullivan cleared his throat, trying to get the words out. "I would *never* do that to anyone. *Ever.*"

"Sullivan, I'm sorry." Lincoln rushed to him, grabbing Sullivan's hands in his own. "I'm so fucking sorry, okay? I was just scared and really worried." He took a breath, holding Sullivan's gaze. "I haven't slept like that since before I went sober, and I panicked. I'm sorry."

Letting his breath out in a whoosh, Sullivan tilted his head back, blinking away the tears. He'd always been teased for having a hair-trigger on his tears, especially when he looked like he could maul a bear. "That really hurt."

His chest ached, the betrayal like a knife in his side. When he looked to the couch, his throat throbbed, his stomach churning uncomfortably.

The strangest part was that Samantha had said worse. At her lowest, she'd called him every name under the sun, cursing him and their friendship. It had hurt, but it hadn't gutted him quite so expertly.

He nearly sobbed as Lincoln wrapped his arms around him, pulling him tight in an embrace that was all friendship and warmth. His head tucked perfectly under Sullivan's chin, his scruff burning against his throat. A tear escaped, despite his best efforts, blazing a trail down his cheek.

"Please forgive me." Lincoln hugged tighter, his own breathing uneven and shallow. When he pulled back, his eyes were shiny and red, the black shadows underneath all but gone.

"I didn't drug you," Sullivan whispered, needing to say it. Lincoln had to know. "I'd never hurt you."

"I know. I'm sorry. Just...let Daddy make it better." It slipped out as if it meant nothing, and Lincoln didn't even seem to notice that he'd said it. Sullivan tensed for a split second before he relaxed into Lincoln's arms.

"Let me make you breakfast," said Sullivan, suddenly too hot and confined. He needed something to occupy his thoughts.

"That's my line, but I'd replace *make* with *order*." Lincoln gave him a soft smile. "There's a mom-and-pop shop downtown that I am absolutely obsessed with. You haven't had Eggs Benedict until you've had theirs. They make their own cheese and everything, and it's divine."

Sullivan shook his head. He probably wouldn't be able to eat, and he didn't want to waste an expensive meal. "Let me cook you something."

"I can go," said Lincoln, squeezing one last time before easing away. Sullivan grabbed him, dragging him close again.

"No, don't go. Just...help me? You can toast the bread and butter it, and I'll scramble up some eggs. It won't take long, and you can use my shower after, if you want."

Hopefully, that didn't sound too desperate. He *had* to keep Lincoln with him until he could show him how good of a man he could be. For Lincoln to think of him so poorly, Sullivan must've given off the wrong vibes. And if Lincoln left now, he was certain that their friendship would crash and burn.

"Okay." Lincoln gave him a soft smile and Sullivan melted. "Someone has to make sure you keep working on your Christmas list."

They made breakfast side by side, Sullivan picking the eggs shells out of the pan after Lincoln enthusiastically wanted to try cracking eggs. Someone arrived halfway through with fresh clothes for Lincoln, which had Sullivan both confused and relieved.

More clothes meant that Lincoln wasn't leaving any time soon, but how did he have someone at his beck and call to deliver them?

"So how rich are you?" asked Sullivan jokingly, plating the last bit of eggs as Lincoln shut the door on his special delivery. There was a spotless suitcase in his hands that was both stylish and appeared to be leather.

"I dunno," said Lincoln absently as he set the case on a chair and unzipped it. He grabbed a pair of thick socks from within, pulling them onto his feet with a sigh. "A few billion maybe? I stopped keeping track after I hit supreme awesomeness."

Sullivan snorted out a laugh, bringing both plates to the table and topping up their glasses—his with orange juice and Lincoln's with straight black coffee. "Maybe I should get into this entrepreneur business, too. I only cleared a million last year."

Now it was Lincoln's turn to laugh. He pointed at the stove with a chuckle. "That thing you call a stove has never seen stainless steel in its life. Where are you hoarding all your cash?'

"Hey, I love my stove." It had...character. In his defense, it had come with the apartment, and it still worked one hundred percent. He'd scrubbed the living daylights out of it when he'd first moved in, and there were a few parts that he'd washed too vigorously so it looked a bit scuffed. "This stove makes the best cookies around.'

"Not according to our conversations. Every time I talk to you, the fucking fire alarm is blaring. I'm surprised you still have a kitchen." He shoved a spoonful of eggs into his mouth, humming appreciatively. "I take it back. This is fantastic."

"My cookies would have turned out fine if you hadn't distracted me." The second it was out, Sullivan flushed and shoveled his own forkful of eggs into his mouth. Lincoln gave him a look, balancing his fork on the edge of his plate.

"How did I distract *you?*" His smirk was almost lecherous.

"Um..." Sullivan took a bite of toast, chewing slowly. It only delayed the inevitable. "You have a nice voice."

That was the understatement of the year. Lincoln could have listed off addresses and Sullivan would have gotten hard. Where was a phone book when he needed one?

"Thank you." Lincoln beamed as he sipped his coffee. "Originally, I was thinking of a sex hotline as a business venture, because I'm just that good, but I feel like that industry is going nowhere these days. This generation barely calls anybody. They'd rather jump straight to the dick pics — and those are free."

As Sullivan finished off and started doing the dishes, Lincoln slid next to him, dipping his hands in the sudsy water until it was up to his elbows. He cursed at how hot it was before grabbing the dishtowel and drying instead.

"You don't have to." Sullivan made a weak grab for the towel, secretly thrilled about the help. After living alone for so long, even the smallest things gave him joy. That, and it was so incredibly domestic that he could almost imagine Lincoln doing it every day.

"This is payment for letting me use your shower after. Full disclosure, I am going to use your body wash because you smell hella good. Also, I *will* wipe my balls on your towel, so you'll have to do an extra load of laundry."

Sullivan swallowed, his mouth suddenly bone-dry. "Or I could just hold onto it for a rainy day."

Lincoln gasped, mock-shocked. "Oh my goodness, your poor husband. It's a wonder he's ever able to leave."

"Yeah, about that—"

"Say no more, Sullivan." Lincoln held up his hand. "Your towel will remain ball-free. I'm sure Loretta packed one for me, anyway. Her attention to detail is second to none. It's too bad she can't read English, because she'd be one hell of a proofreader."

Come on. "But, Lincoln, I don't... I mean, I'm not—"

"I know you don't mind, but I tend to overstep," said Lincoln, hanging the dish towel and grabbing for his suitcase. "Now excuse me, but I'm going to get naked. Feel free to join me." He sent back a wink and a chuckle before he disappeared.

Sullivan grumbled as he drained the water and the distant sound of the shower kicked on. "Maybe I will so you'll listen to me. A guy finally gets the courage to fess up but gets steamrolled by the Lincoln express."

Before his determination could fade, he strode to the bathroom door, carefully testing it in his hand. *Locked.* So Lincoln had been joking again after all.

By the time Lincoln returned to the living room in a cloud of steam and warmth, Sullivan had already cued up the next movie. He'd put fresh snacks and drinks on the table, and he'd found a warmer throw in his closet, which he'd folded on Lincoln's spot. Lincoln eyed it all, giving him a lazy smile.

"You ready to get this show back on the road?" asked Lincoln, taking his seat and instantly burying himself under the blanket.

Sullivan shot him a smirk. "I thought we'd start today off with *Goodfellas*." He showed Lincoln the disc. Lincoln grabbed it in confusion, furrowing his forehead.

"This is not a Christmas movie, Sullivan. It's about the mob!" Lincoln shook his head. "What the hell?"

"This *is* a Christmas movie. The *Frosty the Snowman* song is in it and everything." Grabbing the disc, he shoved it into the player and started it with the remote.

Lincoln grabbed a handful of pretzels. "Next you're going to tell me that *Jaws* is a Christmas movie."

Sullivan gave him a look, scrunching up his nose. "That's about the fourth of July, so no."

Chapter Nine

Three days until Christmas

Three days. Three days of sweet cuddles and domestic bliss before Lincoln had had to leave. They'd watched so many movies that Sullivan's head was a blurry Hollywood mess and had eaten so much takeout that he'd probably gained five pounds.

The gym was calling him, along with the unattended voicemails on his phone, but he was still in a daze. He'd held Lincoln close, soaking up his warmth and basking in his laughter without a single sexual thing passing between them.

Not exactly true. He'd had a boner so long that he'd started to wonder if it was going to stay like that permanently. Luckily, he'd mastered the tuck and hide when he was in high school and Lincoln hadn't mentioned a thing…other than the endless flirting.

Dear me, that man is a tease. Sullivan had spent half his time flushed, loving every second of teasing and silly banter that came so easily between them. And when they'd baked a batch of gingerbread men, Lincoln had decorated their shirts with sayings like 'little slut' and 'eat me, Daddy'. Sullivan had thought he was going to burst into flames, his own gingerbread only wearing ugly festive sweaters of green and red icing.

Grabbing his gym bag, he hefted it over his shoulder, leaving the apartment behind for the first time in days. Next time, he was dragging Lincoln away from the couch and off to the gym. True to his word, the guy hadn't slept a wink on the second night, keeping Sullivan awake with little pokes until he'd passed out for good. When he'd woken, Lincoln had been smiling down at him, his cheeks flushed from the heat of the three blankets wrapped around them.

Was it really the blankets? Sullivan had to keep telling himself that—mostly to keep his sanity, but also to convince his cock to calm down.

The gym was nearly empty when he arrived, and he quickly headed to the changeroom and threw on his sweats and a tight tank that was perfect for when he was lifting. After a quick refresh of his deodorant, he hit the gym floor, heading straight for the treadmill.

Ten kilometers and six hundred lost calories later, he paused for a break, downing an entire water bottle and heading for the rower. His run had left him too shaky for the bench, and he didn't spy anyone that could spot for him. There was another man with biceps twice the size of his, but his stare in the mirror was a touch intimidating.

The man caught his gaze as he glanced over, sending him a wink. His tank must've been a few sizes too small because it rode up his belly, showing off chiseled abs and a treasure trail that would normally have Sullivan drooling.

Sullivan grimaced, turning for the rowing machine. If he wanted to be a guy magnet, he'd hit the free weights or the chin-up bar, but hookups steered cleared of the rower for some reason. Maybe it was all the flailing he did.

He built a steady rhythm, falling into the space between breaths where his muscles burned and every part of his body came alive. His breathing went ragged so much faster than usual, his short stint of laziness and sleeping on the couch taking its toll with stiff muscles and joints.

When he paused for a second break and reached for his refilled water bottle, a muscle in his back panged to life. Grunting, he pushed through it, grabbing the bottle and leaning back onto the machine. His chest heaved as he sucked down water while trying not to choke. Sweat soaked his shirt, already feeling gross in the cool gym.

"You want to spot me, big guy?"

Sullivan grunted at the voice before opening his eyes. It wasn't the intimidating guy he'd expected, but a twink who was maybe half his size. The sweatbands on his wrists and forehead looked fresh from the package, and his pants were tighter than Satan's asshole. He knew well not to judge a book by its cover, though. Samantha could arm curl twenty-five kilograms without breaking a sweat.

"How much are you looking to lift? I pushed myself a bit too much so I'm a tad shaky. I don't think I can help you with more than a hundred." He shook out his hands, quickly wiping the rowing machine down for the next person. When he looked over his shoulder, the guy was staring unashamedly at his ass.

"A hundred pounds?" asked the twink when he was caught. "I don't know if I can do that quite yet. I'm just starting on the 'getting into shape' gig. It's not going very well so far." He pointed to his shin where a red streak was already bruising. "Got that from the free weights."

I meant a hundred kilograms, but sure. He didn't want to emasculate the poor guy, especially when he was trying. Newbies came and went at the gym all the time, but he didn't want to be their reason to leave.

"Let me show you around and give you pointers on some of the machines. It's easy to get hurt if you don't use them correctly — or if you overdo it like I just did." Sullivan grabbed his towel, wiping the sweat from his forehead. His heart was almost beating normally again, and his chest wasn't nearly as tight. If he gave himself a few more minutes, he'd probably get his second wind.

The guy blinked at him before he bit his lip, dragging his gaze up and down Sullivan's torso. His lashes were dark and looked long enough that he was probably wearing mascara. It was a good look for him, but maybe not in a gym. Makeup and sweat did not mix.

I am not in the mood. He was sweaty, tired and horny for another man who was the opposite of a twink. He also didn't have the patience at the moment to even think about this guy.

"Terry! What the hell are you doing?" The twink startled at the shout, spinning toward a man who was running on a nearby treadmill. "I brought you here to get in shape, not blow some guy in the locker room because you want to re-enact a cheap porno."

Terry flushed, whispering out an apology to Sullivan before he jogged over to the treadmills. Starting up his own at a slow walking pace, he glanced back at Sullivan, dragging his tongue over his lower lip.

Do I really want to turn down a blow? He gave Terry and his glaring friend a wave. "You boys have fun!"

He hit the changerooms, showering quickly before pulling on a button-down of his own creation and khakis. He was almost out of the gym before his phone buzzed in his pocket. He glanced at the caller ID, letting out a sigh of guilt when he was disappointed that it was Samantha and not Lincoln.

"Hey, Samantha, what's up?" He headed for his car, shivering as his wet hair instantly froze in the cold. With the wind, it had to have been close to minus twelve centigrade. Christmas was the craziest time of year where he lived. Some years it would be warm enough for shorts, and others it was freezing rain and downright lethal.

"Did I do something?" Samantha asked softly.

"What?" His sneakers crunched on the layer of salt that someone had dumped on the sidewalk. There was a halo of ice and slush around every pile, and his gym shoes were not prepared for it.

"I sent you a text three days ago, but you didn't respond. You didn't even look at the three yesterday either. I know we've been through some rough patches, and I didn't know if I did something or something bad happened. You didn't reply."

Aw, crap. He scratched the back of his head, his freezing fingers snagging on the forming ice. He didn't want to lie, but he didn't exactly want to tell her all about Lincoln either. He had a feeling that she would be pissed if she found out that her elusive pen pal had been in his arms for the last three days. "I was with someone. Sorry."

"*With* someone?" Her voice went high with excitement. "Oh my God, the uncharmable Sullivan finally found a guy who swayed him from single life. Oh! It was that guy on the phone, wasn't it? I knew I shouldn't have let you off so easy. I totally forgive you if you were getting dick downed, though."

"I wasn't getting dick," he whispered, conscious of the lady walking by him. He tossed his bag into his car before ducking into the seat and slamming the door. "We're just friends and there was no sex. Just some snuggling…and movies."

"Not your type?"

Jesus. Lincoln was exactly his type in every way, including the things he had whispered when Sullivan had been pretending to be asleep. Sullivan was a big guy, but that didn't stop him from craving a Daddy or someone he could give himself up to, knowing that they would take care of him.

"I told him I was married." He bit his lip, shaking his head. His breath steamed the air inside the car and he shivered against the cold seat. "I'm so stupid."

"No argument here. Why the hell would you tell him that?"

He gripped the steering wheel, looking out into the wintery landscape. There were people everywhere, and he had so many in his life, but he always seemed to need one more. If he knew every person in the world, he wondered if he would still be lonely.

"I need a friend more than I need a hookup, and I didn't want him to feel pressured into something that's not on the table. Well, it *wasn't* on the table. It would be now if I wasn't such an idiot." Resting his forehead against the steering wheel, he let out a sigh. "I need to get laid."

"Tell me about it...seriously. But not right now. There's an issue with payroll and the bank, which was what I was calling you about. People aren't going to get their Christmas bonuses. If they are half as pissed off as I am, somebody is going to quit."

Sometimes being a COO sucks. Sure, he was paid well enough to live on his own and have a comfortable life with a hell of a retirement savings plan, but when shit went down, he was first on call. The CEO and HR usually looked to him for almost everything.

"Oh crap." He started the car, flipping the call over to Bluetooth. "What happened?" Christmas bonuses were the highlight of the year for some, including himself. He'd already made a few plans for what he was going to do with the money. His new sewing machine would have to wait.

She let out a groan. "Don't ask. Somebody fucked up big time, and right now it looks like there is no fixing it."

Ouch. That sounded bad. "What do you need me to do?"

"Call everybody. I already did a dozen, but I'm hitting a wall, and I know I'm going to say something I regret the next time someone yells at me or cries. I feel like shit, but there's nothing we can do." She let out a choked-off sob.

"Hey. Hey, it's okay. I'll take care of it. Nobody is going to quit." *I hope.* He swallowed. He could think of a few people who were teetering on the edge, their resumes already out to other companies. No matter how hard he tried, he couldn't appease everyone.

"Thanks, Sullivan. I don't know what we'd do without you."

He chuckled. "You got it all wrong, Samantha. Everyone there is like my family. I won't let my family go hungry over the holidays just because the bank made an error. I'll take care of it. And I'll answer the next time you call. I promise."

He rushed home, his mind buzzing with a hundred different call scenarios. His heart hadn't stopped pounding the entire way as he wondered what the hell he would do. If someone was desperate for the money, he had savings that he could use in the interim, but that meant no trip next fall.

He bit his lip. He'd just have to go without. No one was going broke on his watch. The company paid well, but some of the staff were single parents or supported their relatives, not to mention student loans. Not everyone was a single bachelor in a decent place like him.

Three phone calls in, things were starting to look up. He started at the beginning, not knowing who Samantha had already talked to. It turned out that word spread quickly in a workplace that was so tight knit. He was certain there were Facebook groups for entire departments, which was better than any water cooler to get news around.

He dialed Nora's number next, chewing his lip as the phone rang. She was a single mother of three, and her husband had walked out on her when she'd found out she was expecting number four. Sullivan had offered his office as a safe place away from the floor when she had to make private phone calls and had increased the whole company's paid sick leave in case she, or someone else like her, needed it.

"Hey, Nora, I have some bad news," he said as soon as she picked up. He could hear crying in the background, along with the steady noise of shudder-worthy cartoons.

"Oh, damn. I was hoping that it wasn't true. I never know what rumors to believe once they start, but oh shoot." She let out a huff, her voice strained. "I know I shouldn't depend on bonuses for day-to-day items, but things are always short at the end of the year. Everything renews on January first and rent is going up again, too. I just— I haven't got the kids their gifts yet. I know it's cutting things close, but we've been tight. Kelly's sick and little David is getting some molars in, so I hardly have a moment to myself, let alone time to buy presents."

His heart broke a little as she went on. He couldn't imagine how she did it, especially with how exhausted she'd been with her fourth pregnancy so far. She didn't say much at work to anyone else, worried about someone judging her, but Sullivan saw how much of a toll it took on her.

"Text me a list. They'll have their presents, and I'll wrap and deliver them for you." He scribbled down two of the names but couldn't remember the third. He added Nora to the list, too. He could hazard a guess as to when the last time was that anyone had bought her a gift.

"But, Sully—"

"Nope! Sorry, I can't hear you. My Christmas spirit is drowning you out. Seriously, though, Nora, don't worry about it. I don't have any nieces or nephews to buy gifts for, and I'd love to spoil some deserving kids. I do expect a pretty epic hand-drawn picture from Billy, though, as long as he lets his brother and sister help."

He scribbled down the third name. Thank goodness for his memory.

He jotted down a few notes quickly before he forgot. If he remembered right, Billy was at the cowboy stage, and the other two were young enough that they would probably play with the box of whatever they got.

"I don't deserve you, Sully. Jesus." Her thank-you broke down into a quiet sob. "Jesus, thank you."

"No problem." He grinned, the familiar rush of family filling him. It would keep him from missing his parents and Lincoln, hopefully for a while. "What about dinner? Do you have something nice? I have a whole feast in my freezer that I won't be using."

"I couldn't, Sully, no."

"I'll take that as a yes." He added a note so he didn't forget to take the chicken and cranberries over for her. It wasn't a massive bird, but it would probably suit them just fine for one meal. "Unless chicken is making you nauseated right now? Sorry… I didn't think of that."

"It's fine, Sully. Thank you so much."

After a seemingly endless number of 'thank-yous', he finally managed to hang up the phone. He rubbed his neck, crossing her name off his long list. Hopefully, everyone else was set for dinner, because he was fresh out of chickens—and the grocery store probably was, too.

Chapter Ten

"Oh God, that took forever." Sullivan tossed his feet up on the couch, slipping them right into Samantha's lap. She crinkled her nose before pinching his big toe. "Everyone is set, though, and no one is quitting. Crisis officially averted."

He was exhausted, and his neck was beyond strained. The batch of macaroons he'd been planning on making would have to wait. Luckily, Samantha had come over near the end and had helped him power through the last few. His notebook was a full, scribbled mess.

"Want to watch a movie and drink hot cocoa?" Samantha pushed his feet off with one last grimace. "Not sure what you're asking for, but I'm not going to rub those things."

He chuckled, shaking his head. "Honestly? I don't think I ever want to watch another Christmas movie again. I've gone through, like, thirty in the last few days. I need horror or, like, a really good shooting spree to even things out. How about *Starship Troopers*?"

"Gross, no."

His chuckle was cut off as his phone chimed with an incoming call. He let out a groan, throwing himself back onto the couch dramatically. "I can't do one more!"

But I have to. For the good of Christmas! Clearing his throat, he accepted the call.

"Sullivan?"

Butterflies burst in his belly, and he immediately sat up, nearly knocking Samantha from her place. His head spun, his mouth going dry. "Hey! How are you? I missed you."

Oh crap. What am I even saying? Samantha was giving him a knowing look with one brow raised. It had only been hours since he'd last seen Lincoln, and he was being ridiculous. It was high school all over again.

Lincoln let out a low laugh, his voice so rich and deep that it gave him the shivers. "Is it bad if I missed you, too? What can I say? You have a comfy couch...and a comfy lap. I don't think I'll ever sleep that well again."

Sullivan bit his lip, looking at Samantha who was mouthing the same thing over and over—'Tell him.'

"Can we talk about something?" he asked, turning from the couch and heading for the kitchen. He touched his oven mitts that were hanging from the cupboard. Some of the threads were starting to fray. He added them to the to-do list.

"Don't get ahead of yourself, boy. You don't have to be worried. We didn't do anything, and I have no intentions of stealing you from your husband, even if I do think he shouldn't leave such a needy boy alone for so long."

Every *boy* sent a renewed shiver down his spine, his cock awkwardly standing to attention with his best friend only a room away. Did Lincoln even know what he was doing?

"That's the thing... I mean, I'm not—"

"Sullivan, don't worry. You say the word and you'll never see me again. I hope it doesn't come to that, though. Is he giving you issues?"

"Do you ever shut up?" Sullivan couldn't help but snap a bit. His confession had failed nearly a dozen times, and his secret was hanging heavy in his chest. Grabbing the oven mitt, he tossed it to the ground, throwing his frustration along with it.

"Whoa." Lincoln let out a breath. "That's fair, because the answer is no. I'm so tight-lipped around work, but when I'm talking to you, I just can't seem to stop. It's like I'm making up for lost time or something. Sorry, though. I'll do better."

Leaning against his cupboards, Sullivan resisted the urge to bang his head. "Sorry, Lincoln. I've just had a really rough day, and I've been trying to tell you something that I just can't seem to get it out."

"Maybe I can make it better," said Lincoln. Sullivan closed his eyes, listening to the sound of his voice and letting himself get lost. That deep roll had starred in so many dreams in the last few days that he was probably approaching obsessed.

"I know you had your Christmas dinner planned with cranberries and all, but I was wondering if I could steal you away instead. You can freeze cranberries, right? If not, whatever. Nobody likes cranberries."

"I gave my dinner away, actually," said Sullivan, sliding his hand over the counter and pausing on the faux marble. It was cold and dusted with a fine layer of flour that he'd missed when he'd last cleaned it. His ingredients for macaroons were still there, begging to be mixed.

"Of course you did. You'd give your shirt away if you could help someone."

Sullivan chuckled as some of his exhaustion lifted. His shirt was too big to fit most of the people he knew. "Probably, yeah."

"Even more reason to let me treat you to dinner," said Lincoln. "It's not so much dinner as a gala work thing. I'm pretty nervous about it because I can't find a way out of it this year, so I thought I'd take them up on the 'plus one' offer and stir up some shit."

If there was one thing that he'd learned about Lincoln in their brief relationship, other than how he was almost cold-blooded with how many blankets he needed, it was that he loved to make trouble. He didn't always seem to know what to do once he was there, though.

"It's probably best that I go then," he said, a smile on his lips. "Somebody needs to protect you from your consequences."

Lincoln spluttered. "If there's anyone who's going to be doing the protecting, boy, it's me. I don't care if you have a few inches and a wee bit of muscle on me, you're a softie on the inside. Softies don't survive in my kind of business."

Sullivan blinked. So maybe...just maybe, he was a softie, but that didn't make him weak. "I can be hard when I need to be."

He caught Samantha's choked-off laugh from the doorway. He sent her a wink, even as he flushed.

"I'm sure you can, big boy." Lincoln's voice went dark, stripping the humor right from him. "I'll pick you up at six o'clock tomorrow."

Sullivan tossed his phone on the counter when the call ended, closing his eyes and taking a deep breath. It was impossible to ache for someone that he barely knew, right?

Chapter Eleven

Two days until Christmas

As he waited on the curb, he realized that he actually had no idea what kind of car Lincoln would be driving. If it went along with his overly expensive coat, then it would probably be a Corvette or Camaro.

A Toyota looked like it was slowing down, so he stepped closer to the edge of the road, shoving his hands deep in his pockets to keep them occupied. Slush squished from beneath his feet, the salt turning every bit of snow on the sidewalk into a sandy goop.

The Toyota whipped by, catching the edge of his slacks with a drop or two of road debris. He wiped them off quickly, hoping that it didn't show. He pushed for casual at work, and he was almost regretting it since he didn't have anything dressy like a suit in his closet.

Lincoln hadn't given him any clue as to the dress code, and there was nothing worse than being over or underdressed. He'd settled on one of his nicer pairs of slacks and a red dress shirt that Samantha said made him look like a ten. Personally, he thought he was more of a seven-and-a-half, and that was being generous.

His jaw nearly hit the sidewalk when an ominous-looking limo pulled up to the curb before stopping in front of him. He looked around, trying to find someone on the sidewalk that would fit with such a machine. There was no one except Mr. Kippen, who was making his way slowly down the street, his cane clutched in his gnarled hand.

When he looked back to the huge vehicle, the door popped open and Lincoln stepped out.

He looked every inch a man in absolute control who wouldn't be caught dead snuggling on a couch while eating raw cookie dough. Sullivan's mouth went dry as he looked from the shiny dress shoes to the suit that fit Lincoln like a glove. The cuff links shone in the streetlamp with jewels that had to be diamonds laid into them.

It was too much—enough for his brain to stall as he stared. He had no idea how much things like those would cost, but it was so far beyond his reach that it was nearly hilarious. Lincoln must've been going all out to try to impress him.

"Hey, handsome," Lincoln called to him, grimacing as he stepped onto the slushy path. He paused, his expression morphing into panic. "You okay?"

No. A limo? Seriously? Isn't that a bit much for a Christmas party? "I think I'm underdressed." He glanced down at his dress shoes, which were at least two years old. He wasn't hard up for money, but he didn't like to show his paycheck with the value of his clothes or car.

Lincoln gave him one glance before he smiled. Wrapping an arm around Sullivan's shoulders, he pulled him toward the limo. His cologne made Sullivan's mouth water at the same time his cock twitched. He'd missed that scent and the warmth of Lincoln in his home.

"I think you look great. If anyone has an issue with it, I'll just fire them."

"You can't..." His knees went weak, and he fought a shiver. "You can't just fire someone because they disagree with you."

"Sure I can." His smirk was electric. "Now come on. We might as well be early to this thing so we can leave halfway through. I have a date with your couch tonight so I can catch up on my beauty sleep. Then, once I finally shut up, we can talk about whatever it is you wanted to talk about."

Sullivan nodded, allowing himself to be led into the limo. The few limos he had been in during his life had all had the luxurious but run-down feel. The one at his friend Rachel's wedding had been downright trashy. This one was sparkling clean, the seats upholstered with leather that still smelled fresh.

"Did you do this for me?" asked Sullivan once he was finally able to speak. That had to be the reason. Lincoln was just trying to impress him. Maybe he'd already figured out Sullivan's secret and was on the path to woo him.

Lincoln's flush was answer enough. "Maybe. I was just trying to do something nice for you. I feel like you spend a lot of your time treating others, but you don't get spoiled yourself." He leaned into his seat as the car started to move. "So, we've got leather seats, a fully-stocked mini-bar that I'm not touching and a goodie bag that my PA packed for me."

He reached for a shiny red bag that was tucked by the farthest seat, somehow not losing his balance as the car turned. There was a Santa on the package who was astride an obese reindeer that looked like it had hit the eggnog hard.

Sullivan gripped the seat, reaching for a belt and finding none. *So dangerous.* Hopefully, the ride was short.

Lincoln coughed as he opened the bag, slamming it shut and sliding it away. "I think she had the wrong idea when I said I was bringing a friend. I wanted her to get chocolates or something. Not...that."

Sullivan grabbed for the bag despite Lincoln's protests, pouring it out onto the seat. "That's a lot of condoms." There had to be two dozen, along with an assortment of lube. "And is that a candy G-string?" He picked up the package so he could read the label. "One size fits all? Ha!" There was no way his ass would fit into the thing.

"Wait. You're okay with that? My PA thinks I'm some kind of sex fiend and you're laughing?" Lincoln crossed his arms, a smirk on his face. "Where's my blushing boy?"

Sullivan flushed, dropping the G-string back into the bag before trying to sweep the rest inside. One of the condoms escaped, sliding across the floor of the limo. "It *is* funny. And it's good to be prepared. You never know who you're going to offer a hand job to outside of random apartment buildings."

Lincoln snickered, shuffling across the seat until their shoulders were pressed together. He threw his arm around Sullivan, tugging him close. "You're never going to let me live that down. I finally step off my solo soapbox, and the first guy I try to pick up is my new pen pal. Figures."

Lincoln pulled away as the car rolled to a stop, grabbing for the door and tugging it open. "Oh, thank Christ, nobody is here yet. Let's hurry before we get mobbed or something." He reached back, helping Sullivan from the car like a gentleman.

"Oh my." Sullivan looked up, then looked higher. "Is this the right place?"

There was one place in town he knew he would never be able to afford. *The Royale* was one of the hottest and hippest places on the continent, but it catered to rich businessmen and kids with trust funds. Not someone like him.

Black gates surrounded the entrance and a red carpet peeked through the front door. A doorman dressed all in white was ready to greet them, the buttons on his shirt nearly luminous. The pictures that circulated online didn't do the place justice.

The limo pulled away and Lincoln hooked his arm through Sullivan's. "Shall we?"

Brakes! He locked his knees, looking at his attire. His coat was a bit frayed around the edges because he was waiting for the next fabric sale before he made a new one. That, along with his casual clothes hidden underneath, and he would stick out like a sore thumb. Lincoln's lack of a coat and his suit suddenly made perfect sense.

"There's no way that I can afford this place." His heart pounded, his mouth going dry as a headache throbbed into existence. *How embarrassing.* "Can we go somewhere else?" He wasn't even making sense, but he couldn't go into that place. People like him didn't belong.

Lincoln's hand dropped to his, and he squeezed so hard it almost hurt. He'd pressed his lips into a serious line, his eyes laser-focused on Sullivan. "I may not be able to do everything I want with you, but let me do this. I promised to treat you and I will. Don't worry about it anyway. I know a guy who knows a guy."

His knees were officially weak. He gripped Lincoln's hand, for fear he'd drop to the ground if he let go. Lincoln was right. No one had spoiled him in his life, except perhaps his parents. That thought had him close to tears. *Relax.*

"Okay. But if somebody makes fun of my clothes, I may have to punch them." That was a total lie. He'd never punched someone in his life. He'd never had to, either. They usually backed down the moment they saw him frown.

A man greeted them at the entrance, smiling at Lincoln as if they were friends. "We have your seating for you and your guest arranged, sir, and the sound system has been set up in the great hall. You have a few minutes before the guests arrive if you wish to make any changes."

"I'm sure it's all good. I trust you, man." Lincoln sent him a wink before dragging Sullivan into the building.

Every hair on his body stood on end at once as richness washed over him. Somehow, it had a smell — clean and deep with a twist that made him wonder what it could have been. Every surface gleamed, from the meandering staircase to the actual chandelier just inside.

Another person greeted them inside the door, whisking them through a few elaborate hallways before they arrived at a set of French doors that a giant could have walked through. They were made of solid wood, the surface carved into a thousand figures that were stained dark.

When they opened, Sullivan nearly fainted. Gripping Lincoln's hand tight, he stepped inside.

It was a winter wonderland, with sparkling lights, crisp decorations and more tables than he could count. Each was dressed in gold cloth with sparkling place settings and dusted cedar boughs. It was like stepping into a fantasy of the most expensive Christmas wedding in the world. Butlers rushed about, each dressed in the same white uniform as the doorman. There wasn't a wrinkle between them or a hair out of place.

"I..." Sullivan couldn't speak. There was no way that this was all for him, too. There was something he was missing. Something big.

"Your seat is this way, sir." One of the butlers stepped forward, greeting Lincoln with a small bow. The silver plate in his hand was polished and bright and he even *smelled* like peppermint.

Who fucking bows?

Lincoln looked at him, a tension in his shoulders weighing heavily. The sight of it shocked something in Sullivan's core, bringing him back to the present. His ears still rang, but Lincoln was his focus and not the fake snow dusting from the ceiling into piles about the periphery where a life-sized nativity scene shone in gold and silver.

"Is it okay? I may have told them to go a bit overboard with the decorations, but I wanted it to be nice. It's not every day I get to take my new best friend out for dinner."

"How rich are you?" Sullivan asked, swallowing the confusion that threatened to drag him into silence. He was certain that he'd asked Lincoln that before, and what had he said? A few billion? He'd thought that had been a joke.

Lincoln shrugged, a frown tugging at his lips. "Does it matter?"

Sullivan shook his head so fast that the room spun. "No. Not at all. You're still the same guy who fell asleep on my lap with a pretzel in your hair. I just...I thought you were joking."

His heart pounded. He'd snuggled with a billionaire? One had been in his house and his shower where some of the tiles were broken and others were overdue for a spring cleaning? He needed to clean his condo *now*.

"Nah." Lincoln shook his head, tugging Sullivan along as their butler paused to wait for them. "I'm rich as fuck. I joke about it because it makes people uncomfortable sometimes. I wanted you to be comfortable with me. I hope this doesn't change things."

A sparkling white tree stood in their path and it took Sullivan a moment to realize that it was real. The scent of pine was thick in the air, a few needles on the carpet below. Someone had painstakingly painted each needle, getting every bit until it appeared white. There were boxes at the base wrapped in gold ribbon and stacked in cute arrangements.

"It doesn't."

The tension eased and Lincoln gave him one of his devilish smirks that was full of unfulfilled promises. "Good."

It doesn't? Sullivan tried to stop gawking, but he couldn't. His neck was getting sore from whipping his head around, but everywhere he looked, he found something he hadn't noticed before—like the ice sculpture of a frozen fountain near the door that slowly dripped into an array of crystal glasses.

They stopped at a table that was just a touch grander and larger than those around it. There were two place settings across from each other with silver charger plates and glossy napkins shaped into roses. The surrounding tables all had at least ten place settings and the napkins were adorned with simple rings.

Lincoln released him, grabbing one of the chairs and dragging it all the way around the table until it was next to the other. The butler rushed along with the rest of the place setting, rearranging it before sweeping the tablecloth with a small brush he produced from his jacket. "There. That's better. I don't want to have to shout at you all through dinner."

Sullivan nodded, his tongue still partially glued to the roof of his mouth. He touched the fork, the utensil heavy in his palm. They were like the ones in the china shop that his mother had absolutely adored.

"You still seem starstruck," said Lincoln as he helped Sullivan into his chair, tucking it in tightly as Sullivan collapsed into it. "I'm still the same man, I promise."

His blue eyes were so captivating, and the sensual curve of his mouth drew Sullivan in like no other. *Soon.* "I'm always starstruck around you. Sometimes I can hardly speak because I'm too busy just looking at you and listening."

If he said anything more, he would be stepping into stalker territory. It was probably best not to mention that watching Lincoln sleep was one of the most relaxing things in the world—better than puppy yoga even.

Lincoln said something under his breath before grabbing Sullivan's glass and filling it for him like a gentleman. Sullivan took a sip, wincing at how cold the water was. Even *it* tasted expensive, with a touch of lemon and something else citrusy.

"Don't whisper around me," said Sullivan, looking toward the door as someone new appeared. "I promise I won't judge. What did you say?" There wasn't much that Lincoln *could* say to turn him off. Now that his sights were firmly fixed, he wasn't backing down. Every cell in his body was going for the guy.

"Nah, you'll get upset. I shouldn't have said anything out loud to begin with." He grabbed his glass of water, taking a sip before motioning to one of the butlers. "Sullivan, were you going to have some wine?" He motioned to the two bottles on ice near the center of the table.

Sullivan hoped against hope to be doing some kissing later and he didn't want to trigger Lincoln with any taste on his tongue. He'd give up beer for the rest of his life if it meant one kiss — even the homebrew recipe that had taken three times to get right.

"No thank you."

The light of a smile touched Lincoln's eyes, and he leaned his elbow on the table, resting his chin on his palm.

"I don't mind. That bottle is some kind of three-hundred-dollar beast that I can't pronounce." He reached for it, showing Sullivan the label.

Grapes weren't exactly high on his knowledge list, and he only ever drank wine when he was out with Samantha anyway. Lincoln was right, though. He had no idea how to pronounce *Chateau d'Yquem Sauternes*.

"I can't wait to kiss you," he whispered under his breath so Lincoln had no chance of hearing him. "I'll pass." He spoke up, smiling at the twinkle in Lincoln's eyes.

"Give this to someone who wants it," said Lincoln as he handed off the bottle to the butler who gave a little bow. "And that one, too." He pointed to the red bottle with the label that appeared antique.

People started to filter into the hall, catching Sullivan's eye every time. A woman appeared in an ankle-length dress that was slit all the way to her mid-thigh. It shimmered every time she moved, like a dazzling snowstorm around her body. The man beside her wore an expensive suit with a red shirt underneath that looked like silk.

Sullivan peered at his own clothes. Lincoln had passed his coat off to a butler and he'd felt naked ever since. There was even a wrinkle across his belly that hadn't been there when he'd put it on.

"You look wonderful," said Lincoln, as if noticing his unease. "The difference between their beauty and yours is that yours comes naturally, but they have to spend hours trying to come close. And besides, even if you weren't the most attractive man I know, you're still the best one."

His breath caught and he reached for Lincoln's hand, squeezing once. Conversations picked up around them as the hall filled to capacity, but he could barely hear them.

"I need to tell you now." Sullivan squeezed his hand harder, terrified that Lincoln would pull away. "Please." He needed to kiss him, even if it was in front of a hundred strangers. There were probably more than that, most of them looking their way with something akin to hushed curiosity.

"Of course, I—"

A loudspeaker cut him off, a small burst of feedback sending the hall into silence. Off to the side of their table, a woman who Sullivan hadn't noticed tapped a microphone before she started to speak.

"Thank you everyone for coming tonight. It's so great to see you outside the office, especially you, Mr. Shelby." She looked to their table.

She kept talking as Sullivan turned, and he glanced behind him to try to figure out who she was speaking to. His heart thudded and his palms started to sweat when he realized that there was no one in that section but them.

"That's my PA Debra. She's such a brat sometimes. She just had to rub it in that this is the first gala I've made it to in ten years." Lincoln tugged his hand free to cross his arms, setting his face in a stern glare. Every bit of easiness and relaxation was gone.

"*You're* Mr. Shelby? I mean, Lincoln Shelby?" Sullivan choked halfway through, drawing the gazes of a few people at nearby tables. He was sure that he was pale or bright red but wasn't sure which. Terror and surprise were doing terrible things to him.

Lincoln nodded once, his lips pressed in a thin line before he spoke softly. "Am I still the same man?"

It wasn't so much a question as a barbed accusation. Sullivan shook his head, everything around him swimming in and out of focus.

Lincoln Shelby was the richest man in the country and one of the top one hundred richest in the world. He was a renowned businessman who took out his competition with ruthless accuracy. There wasn't a person on the planet who didn't know his name, and for each one who benefited from his work, another ten despised him.

Sullivan had been among those ten—at least, he'd thought he had been. But he'd always pictured a faceless multi-billionaire with an ego that would never fit in a gorgeous suit. He'd never thought of the mogul as a man before.

But Lincoln Shelby was *his* Lincoln, the man who fell asleep on his lap and whispered in his dreams—the man who was passionate, funny and sweet, and who couldn't cook worth a shit.

"How— Why didn't you tell me?" Sullivan gripped the napkin, his hands going cold as sweat dripped down his back. "You kept joking about money so I wouldn't take you seriously, but now I find out who you really are?"

"It shouldn't matter." Lincoln's voice had gone cold, just a tad louder than it needed to be. The woman at the podium paused, looking their way.

"Mr. Shelby, would you like to say anything?" she asked.

Lincoln grabbed his glass, taking a sip before pushing his chair back. He strode to the podium like a predator, his body tense and ready to pounce on the nearest underling that stepped out of line. The silence in the room was complete, with every bit of laughter sucked from it.

Should I leave? I should leave. Sullivan pushed his chair back, every eye pressing into him from all around. It had probably just been a fun game for Lincoln—a distraction from his money, fame and business. But for Sullivan, it had been everything, even if he'd kept a secret of his own.

Lincoln took the stand before Sullivan could move, the microphone screeching as he grabbed it and tugged it toward his mouth. Disconnecting it from its mount, he strode back to their table, leaning against the edge. It blocked Sullivan's view of the exit and his hope of escape.

"I'd say welcome, but I don't want to lie to everyone," said Lincoln, his deep voice crashing through the speakers in the silent room. A few people fidgeted in their expensive clothes, some reaching for their wine glasses. "You see, I usually hate these things. The dinner, the dressing up and the drinking make me want to hide my head in the sand. I mean, I wear a suit to work every day. Why the hell would I want to wear one for Christmas?"

He paused, letting the silence stretch.

Sullivan swallowed, looking up at Lincoln. Lincoln was trembling, his grip white-knuckled on the tablecloth. Even in his expensive suit with his hair perfectly in place and billions of dollars at his beck and call, he was still shaking.

Lincoln was right. He was still the same man, and that was all that mattered.

Sullivan reached for him, brushing his knuckles over the back of Lincoln's hand. Lincoln let out a breath, relaxing his shoulders as a smile touched his lips. It was almost painful to watch.

"You can call me Scrooge or Grinch, but I've always hated Christmas. It was a good excuse for an extra drink, but that's about it." Lincoln turned his hand, grasping Sullivan's in his own. "But this year has been a bit different—a lot different. Some of you know about my stint in rehab, and for most, it didn't come as a big surprise. I'm four years sober tonight, which is the best anniversary I've ever had. I wanted to celebrate it with the people I've come to love and trust."

There was a look between them, so brief that Sullivan wasn't sure if he imagined it. The squeeze against his hand wasn't his imagination, though, or the way Lincoln had started to tremble again.

Lincoln was afraid. He was fucking terrified, but Sullivan wasn't sure if he was projecting or if it was what he was really seeing.

"You probably don't believe me, but I trust every single person in this room—except maybe Debra." He sent his PA a smirk, and a few chuckles broke out. "If I didn't trust you, you wouldn't be working with me. Everyone here is important in their own right, and none of us would be able to do our jobs without you. Michael"—he gestured to a terrified-looking man who appeared as if he were barely out of his teens—"if you didn't do your job to perfection, none of us would have our mail on time. The last time I opened someone else's mail, I ended up with a dildo on my desk...Debra."

He shot her another sly grin, and she spluttered.

"Just kidding, Debra. You know I love you. But, Michael, you are just as important and trustworthy as Jim." He gestured to a balding man who held his head high and his wine glass higher. "Jim, you had what? Twenty-four million in commission this year? Not something to scoff at. You're our highest earner in the room besides myself, and you are just as irreplicable as Michael."

Lincoln tapped the microphone against his chin. "You might be surprised to learn that I know every single one of you. I've gone years without speaking to most of you, and I was completely fine with that...until someone managed to show me the error of my ways."

He squeezed Sullivan's hand again, a pulsing beat beneath the tremble.

"So, I'm going to be changing a few things around the office. For one, I'm not making a single budget cut this year, and that includes the office supplies you guys so desperately horde." He chuckled at Debra's frown. "Honestly, if you guys wanted a dozen extra pens, you only had to ask."

A few whispers of movement and laughter circulated.

"Other things will change, too." He let out a long breath, staring straight at Sullivan.

Sullivan's heart pounded as he met Lincoln's gaze. Every eye in the room was on him, but he only needed two.

"I'm going to take a step back," said Lincoln, bringing Sullivan's hand to his lips and placing a single kiss that was amplified across the speakers. "And I don't expect a single person to take my place. Three days of vacation and I'm more rested than I've been in twenty years."

He glanced to Debra, who gave him a look full of confusion and worry. Pulling the microphone away, he whispered, 'I'm not drunk. Don't worry' to her.

"Effective tonight, I'm doubling everyone's vacation time, and it's going to be mandatory. I'm looking at you, Bill. Deadlines aren't everything, and I think we need to work on that as a whole this year. If you have any concerns or something you think we can do better, my door is open to you during office hours. Other than that...well, Merry Christmas."

Debra grabbed the microphone from him with a look of mild alarm mixed with the touch of joy that had surrounded every person in the room. Lincoln slid back into his seat, a smile on his lips as he squeezed Sullivan's hand tight.

"Thank you, sir, for that...uh...interesting update," said Debra, heading back to the podium. "And without further ado, let's eat."

Chapter Twelve

"That was a nice speech," said Sullivan as the butlers started handing out small plates with some kind of appetizer that looked like foam. Lincoln dipped his spoon into it, sucking it from his utensil like a kid with chocolate milk.

"I thought you were going to leave," said Lincoln, not looking up from his food. Licking his spoon clean, he set it on the table, dragging his fingertips over the cloth.

"I thought so, too," said Sullivan honestly. He wasn't going to lie about it—not when there was already a big barrier to come down between them. He was still only a step away from running out of the door, ready to spook at the smallest thing.

The foam was citrusy and light, barely coating his tongue before it was gone. His stomach rumbled in protest. "I may have overreacted a bit, but I was startled, I guess. It's not every day that I find out someone I know is a secret billionaire. I'm sorry for how I reacted, Lincoln. It was uncalled for."

Lincoln curled the edges of his lips, resting his chin on his hand as he leaned one elbow on the table. "I didn't try to keep anything a secret. You're just oblivious."

"Ouch." *Damn, I want to kiss him so bad.* He was close enough that Sullivan could lean forward and their lips would touch. But they were also at a work function where everyone seemed to be watching them.

"Is there any real food coming?" Sullivan asked instead as he caught sight of a second round of dishes with green foam on their way. It was no wonder rich people managed to stay so skinny. Lincoln's eyes lit up before he waved down one of the butlers.

"I want a steak for my boy here — at least twelve ounces — with a side of asparagus and mashed potatoes. Cook it medium-rare."

Sullivan flushed, biting his lip. No one had ever ordered for him, but he had to admit that it was pretty fantastic — except for the medium-rare part. "Make it medium-well, please, but everything else is okay."

Lincoln raised one brow, ignoring the butler as he stumbled through some type of excuse for not having steak prepared immediately. "I always took you for a rare kind of guy. You eat raw cookie dough."

Sullivan chuckled, giving the flustered butler an apologetic look. "That was your idea, Lincoln. I much prefer my cookies baked and salmonella-free."

"Pah, you worry too much." Lincoln waved him off, grabbing his water and taking a sip. "I always eat it raw, and I'm fine."

Sullivan's mind dropped straight to the gutter. He would love it if Lincoln took him raw, too. He shook his head, trying to avoid getting hard. "It literally says on the package not to eat it uncooked. But you were right.

It tastes way better. Everything in life is better raw." *Oops.*

Lincoln's gaze went dark. "You're really asking for it. Just what am I going to do with you?"

Sullivan struggled to nod, his heart in his throat. Whatever Lincoln gave him, he wanted it to be a surprise. Surprises were the spice of life.

"If you want to see me dance around this all night, boy, you're going to be disappointed." He leaned in, the scent of his cologne stripping the last of Sullivan's defenses. "You would do anything I asked, wouldn't you?"

It sounded like more of an accusation than a question, but the answer was still the same. *Yes.*

"What would he say if he saw you here with me? Looking at me the way you are, you're asking for it...you want it. Maybe it would turn him on to see you with another man, or maybe it would just piss him off because you're only like this for *me*."

Sullivan's brain took another holiday and he clung to the table. *He's talking about my non-existent husband.* He'd needed a fake divorce for far too long.

"He's not—"

"I don't want to know. I was trying to hold myself back, but I've had a wonderful idea that is so much better." Lincoln clenched his fists as if hardening his resolve. "When you are here with me, you're mine and only mine. Who do you belong to right now?"

Holy fuck. His heart was about to beat out of his chest. There were people all around them that could probably hear every word if they cared to. To think that Lincoln had been holding back all along had his cock hard despite his efforts.

"You." Lincoln's eyes looked almost black when Sullivan finally said it. His ears roared as he slid their palms together, both smooth and soft from a life in the office. "Are we dating?"

Lincoln chuckled, a low thing that promised so much more than just pleasure. "Sure, boy. I can be your Daddy, since you asked so nice. Now eat your steak, and if you're good, I'll give you a reward."

Sullivan blinked and the steak was before him, looking like a monstrosity next to Lincoln's green soup that was swirled with something orange. He cut into it automatically, numbly answering the butler as he asked if it was prepared to his liking. He couldn't look away from Lincoln.

My Daddy?

He'd explored kink during some of his relationships, but he'd never confessed his secret hope for a Daddy who would look after him. His dynamic with previous partners had never been what he and Lincoln had, though. With other men, there was always something forced and uneven. Most twinks just wanted to climb him like a tree, and the bigger guys wanted to Dom the fuck out of him, giving him more than he could take.

"Where did you go?" asked Lincoln, touching his chin and dragging Sullivan's gaze back to him. "Is my boy okay?"

"Yeah, just thinking." Sullivan took a deep breath, staring at his steak that was somehow already half-gone. Lincoln's soup had been replaced with a salad that had leaves in colors that Sullivan had never seen. "I've never had a Daddy before—not a real one. There were a couple of guys who tried, but we never matched well. I'd really like it if you were my first real one."

Lincoln's grin was predatory. "Too bad your first Daddy has to be a secret one, hmm? I'll take care of you, boy. You'll want for nothing."

Sullivan shook his head. "That's not what I meant." It was so important for him to get it out and off his chest before it smothered him. "I don't want anything… I just want you. You're enough."

Lincoln drew away suddenly, his face closing off until he was completely unreadable. Sullivan's heart thundered, aching with how hard it was beating. It was the same face that he'd seen when he'd been ready to run from the hall.

"Did I say something wrong?" asked Sullivan, his voice sounding pathetic, even to his own ears. Maybe it was too much—the pretend husband, the secrets and not wanting monetary gifts. Maybe he wasn't worth it.

"I think it's time for us to leave," said Lincoln, standing abruptly and leaving the rest of his salad behind. He looked to the butler who approached them with a strained expression. "Bring me his coat and get the limo out front. We're leaving."

Sullivan looked at the steak on his plate where there was enough for another meal. He almost had a phobia about throwing away food, and always tried repurposing it or keeping leftovers so nothing went to waste.

"And wrap my boy's meal up. I won't have him going hungry just because I'm in a rush."

The butler scurried away, and Lincoln leaned over the back of Sullivan's chair, his lips beside Sullivan's ear.

"You didn't do or say anything wrong, boy, but you made Daddy very impatient. Don't think you'll get away with rushing me. I plan to savor every inch of you, despite what you may think about it."

Sullivan was barely able to hold onto his small takeaway container as they left the hall in a hush of whispers that buzzed against his ears. He only had eyes for one man, and he was the most impeccably dressed of them all.

He swore there was a flash of light as they stepped into the limousine, the driver shutting the door behind them. The silence was thick beneath the soft sound of the engine and his own heart. His hands trembled, his pants so tight that he was surprised he hadn't passed out. He'd never wanted someone so badly before.

But Lincoln slid across the limousine, taking the farthest seat and leaning back. He spread his legs wide, resting his arms on either side and effectively taking up the entire seat. Sullivan had the strangest urge to drop his food and go to his knees right there.

"Sit there." Lincoln pointed to the opposite side as if he knew exactly what Sullivan was thinking. Maybe it was plain as day on his face.

"I need to talk to you," said Sullivan, reluctantly sitting as the car started to roll. His food slipped from his hand, landing top-first on the ground. Luckily, there was some fancy folding that kept it all in place.

"I promised I would listen, but as I recall, I said after dinner when we were back at your place. I'm not sure if you'll want to talk then." Lincoln shrugged with one shoulder, tapping the seat and looking toward the closed divider. "Unless you want me to stop. Say the word and I'll stop. I'd never force you into anything."

Sullivan grimaced at the thought. "As if you could."

Luckily, other than keeping an eye on his drinks at the bar, he'd never had to worry that someone would take advantage of him. Most guys were too intimidated to try, and the ones who weren't got a lesson or two in manners.

"You don't think I could?" Lincoln laughed. "With one word, I could have you on your knees and be so far down your throat you'd never talk right again. I know you would listen, even if you didn't want to."

He's right. Sullivan swallowed, plucking at a tab on his container.

"I need you to tell me to stop if it's too much. I need to trust that you will, because until you do, I will do everything in my power to make sure that you'll never forget me."

The limo rolled to a stop much sooner than Sullivan would have thought. The drive to the hall had felt so much longer, and the air hadn't been nearly as thick.

"Last chance, Sullivan. Invite me upstairs and I'll show you what it's like to be my boy. If you ask me to stay here instead, you'll have a friend for life, but I'll never touch you again. I wouldn't be able to without trying to kiss you before I stole you away from *him*." He grimaced at the last word, as if it were foul on his tongue.

Sullivan would tell him—he had to—but he also didn't want to risk the hottest thing in his life coming to an end. His lie was heavy and unyielding, but it could wait another day. His cock couldn't.

"Do you want to come up for a cup of coffee and a movie?"

Lincoln smiled, leaning across the small space. "I thought you'd never ask."

Chapter Thirteen

"Did you want a coffee or something?" asked Sullivan as he stepped into his apartment. Lincoln had barely eaten anything for dinner before they'd left, unless foam and salad counted.

He got the words out a second before his back hit the wall. Letting out a groan, he looked down at Lincoln, whose eyes were blazing, his face set with serious intent.

"It's my turn to look after you now," said Lincoln, his voice a low growl. He threaded his hands through Sullivan's hair, pulling him down and bringing their lips together.

Sullivan let out a gasp, opening his mouth for Lincoln as soon as they touched. Lincoln was warm, soft and hard in all the right ways, his mind swimming and his cock throbbing in seconds. Lincoln was assertive, but he didn't force Sullivan into submission. Instead, he merely convinced him with his tongue to follow along.

Knees trembling, he grabbed at Lincoln's shoulders, sucking in a breath through his nose as the kiss deepened into something that couldn't be called innocent. The sound of their spit sliding together was louder than his pounding heart—and so much dirtier. He swallowed, sucking as much of Lincoln down as he could.

Way too soon, Lincoln pulled back, keeping Sullivan pinned with a gentle hand to his chest. His lips were swollen and dark red, and his chin was irritated from Sullivan's beard. It was a great look on him...maybe even better than the suit.

"You're beautiful," said Sullivan, trying to reach for a second kiss, only to have Lincoln chuckle and push him to the wall.

"I'll take that coffee now. Bring it to the bedroom when you're ready to be a good boy for me."

Sullivan didn't bring food or drinks into his bedroom *ever*, unless he was sick and he needed a glass of water. He wasn't about to complain, though.

Lincoln slipped off his shoes and disappeared into the condo, flicking on lights as he went while Sullivan darted for the coffee machine and turned it on. It was the first time he had ever cursed not having a Keurig that would have had the cup ready in forty-five seconds. The suspense was killing him, and the kiss had only made him hungrier.

The moment the coffee was done, he rushed to the bedroom, flinging the door open from where it was only cracked. His breath caught in his throat as he took in the sight of Lincoln on his bed. He wasn't naked—quite the opposite, in fact—but it was everything he'd imagined. His hair was light against the purple pillow, the top button of his suit undone to show off a patch of dark chest hair speckled with gray. He was every inch the silver fox Sullivan had first pegged him for.

"Like what you see?" asked Lincoln, running his own hand down his chest before sitting up and dangling his legs over the side.

Sullivan nodded, his tongue unable to function. Handing the coffee over, he took a step back, biting his lip as Lincoln took a small sip. Butterflies bounced around his stomach as if they were on crack, throwing him for yet another loop. *It's just Lincoln. He's still the same man.* The number of zeros behind his name didn't matter in the bedroom, but it sure didn't help his nervousness.

"It's perfect. You know just how I like it." He grabbed a tissue, placing it on the nightstand before he set the cup on top. "How is it that you managed to get it perfect? Even Debra struggles with that most days."

"Um." *Is that a rhetorical question?* "I put a touch of tap water in to cool it down so you could drink it right away, and I bought the flavored creamer that you mentioned the other day. Thought I would surprise you with it. Plus, there's an added secret in there that I'll take to my grave." *It sounds nasty when I say it like that.* "It's cinnamon."

Lincoln chuckled, shaking his head. "You got it all wrong, Sullivan. You got it perfect because *you* are perfect. You're such a good boy. I just wish you knew it, too."

Warmth flooded his belly and for some reason, he had the strangest urge to cry. He fisted his hand in his pants instead, his knees wobbling.

"Get on your knees, boy. I'm going to drink my coffee and you're going to show me how perfect you are with that mouth of yours." Lincoln tugged the button on his suit pants, easing the zipper open with one hand. He reached for the coffee with the other, taking a sip with a soft sigh.

Sullivan went to his knees, the laminate flooring harsh against him. He was already drifting to a place he'd never been, so focused on his goal that he didn't care to give it a name.

"Here." Lincoln passed him a pillow from the bed. "You can ask for things so you're comfortable. I want you to be comfortable—well, unless you're being punished. Have you ever been punished before, Sullivan?"

His face burned as his hands shook. Sliding the pillow under his knees, he let out a sigh of absolute relief. It would have been fine if he were in his twenties, but those years were long since passed. "I've never had a relationship like this before. I've always wanted to be good for my Daddy, but most guys don't exactly give it their all." A thought wormed into his mind, and he couldn't hold it back. "But I won't *need* to be punished if I'm perfect."

Lincoln blew the steam in his cup, sipping and swallowing. He didn't react as Sullivan tugged his pants wider, reaching for the prize within and pulling it into the open air.

"Perfection is overrated." With his free hand, he grabbed the back of Sullivan's head, tugging his mouth straight down.

Choking, Sullivan resisted the urge to withdraw, swallowing instead and tonguing over the head of Lincoln's cock. It was a good size, his lips stretched wide around the uncut head. The velvety skin lured him closer as he swallowed the taste, seeking more as if it were the perfect drug.

"Too much?"

Sullivan shook his head as much as he could.

"Good. You take my cock so well, boy. Take it deeper. Tap my thigh if you need a break."

Lincoln tugged him closer, his cock hitting the back of Sullivan's throat and bringing a gag from deep within him. Sullivan fought it down, tears streaming from his eyes as he struggled to take more. It was impossible. It had been too long since he'd properly deepthroated someone, and he was far out of practice.

He tapped Lincoln's thigh, sucking in a breath when he was immediately released. His face flamed with shame as he let out a cough. A simple blow job and he'd already failed.

"You okay?" Concern crept into Lincoln's voice as he set his cup on the tissue. It had to be almost empty.

Sullivan nodded, rubbing his neck where he could still feel the phantom cock filling him. It was okay, just so far out of his league he wasn't sure what he was supposed to be doing. "Maybe just slow down a bit? It's been a long time for me."

"Of course." Lincoln patted the bed beside him. "Let's talk for a minute and reboot."

Sullivan dragged himself onto the bed, grateful for the pillow that had been beneath his knees. Without it, he wouldn't have made it off the floor without a hell of a lot less grace.

"What do you like?" asked Lincoln, tucking himself back into his pants.

Now that just won't do. Sullivan wasn't *exactly* submissive. He liked to push, but he also liked to blush. Taking his partner off guard was his real cup of tea.

Sliding his hand across the blankets, he rested it on Lincoln's thigh. Lincoln tensed beneath his hand, his muscles twitching. He didn't look it, but he must've been just as nervous as Sullivan.

But Sullivan had something on his side. He'd been dreaming about exactly what he wanted to do with Lincoln almost since their first letter.

He brought their lips together, moving slow so Lincoln would have the chance to pull away. He didn't, cupping the back of Sullivan's neck and tilting his head into the touch. Suddenly, he was drowning, with Lincoln on his tongue and inside his mouth as they moved together.

Sullivan used every trick he'd ever learned, tracing Lincoln's mouth and playing with his tongue then drawing him in and sucking before scraping his teeth over Lincoln's lower lip. Lincoln shuddered, wrapping his arms tighter and tilting them until Sullivan's back hit the bed. He sank into the mattress with a sigh, Lincoln's weight holding him steady.

"Much better," said Lincoln as he pulled back, scraping his fingers through Sullivan's beard. Sullivan let out a groan, his toes curling as he leaned into the touch. "I've never been with a bearded man before. It's softer than I expected, and it sure beats a prickly five-o'clock shadow."

Sullivan grunted, gasping as Lincoln kissed down his neck until he touched his collar. It was one of his most sensitive areas, and each touch sent a surge of lust straight to his gut. He had to be tenting his slacks, because his boxers were already slick with pre-cum.

"You remember when I told you that I'm a nipple man?" Lincoln flicked two buttons free, moving onto the third that was level with Sullivan's nipples. "I can't wait to see yours—and taste them. You are so sweet."

Lincoln moved with sure strokes, untucking Sullivan's shirt and undoing the rest of the buttons in only a few seconds. The first touch of his warm hands to Sullivan's chest was nearly his undoing. Sullivan surged, bucking his hips in search of friction as his nipples were caressed.

"And isn't this the best surprise," said Lincoln, rolling his thumbs over the piercings through Sullivan's nipples.

He'd always considered his belly button to be his most sensitive area, next to his cock, but apparently, he'd been severely misguided. Lincoln's fingers were like fire against his pert buds, and when he finally lowered his lips to suck, teeth clicking against metal, it was as if he were drowning.

"M-more. Please, Lincoln." He grasped the back of Lincoln's head, pressing his face firmer into his pec as Lincoln sucked and scraped his teeth over one nipple before diving for the next. Sullivan started to ache, the sensations so foreign that he wasn't sure how much more he could take.

"You like that, boy?"

Sullivan nodded, whining in the back of his throat as Lincoln bit down enough to send the ache wavering closer to pain. Soothing licks were next, before the sucking started all over again. He throbbed, the piercings making him that much more sensitive.

"I-I can't." He was so close to coming that his balls were drawing up, his inevitable end looming closer. He'd never come untouched before, and definitely not from his nipples alone.

"So fucking good for me. Show me that you're mine and hold on just a little bit longer." Lincoln sucked again, flicking his tongue against the swollen bud that was so sensitive it made a whole new sensation start to build.

"Daddy, please," Sullivan begged, gripping the sheets and nearly tearing them from the bed as he tried to hang on. "*Please.*"

A moment later, Lincoln's mouth was gone, his soft breath tickling over his stomach instead. He was curled over himself, one hand on Sullivan's side and the other lost between his own legs. *Oh, God, he's touching himself.*

Lincoln looked up, his cheek against Sullivan's belly. "You are so fucking amazing. Why did I wait this long? You're beyond anything I could have imagined."

Sullivan bit his hand to hold back his scream as Lincoln dipped his tongue deep into his belly button. His nerves flared, his cock pulsing as he came in his boxers, his balls aching from the force of his orgasm. His spine snapped taut, and something tore above his head.

When he looked over, he saw the tattered remains of his sheets in his hand.

Lincoln laughed as Sullivan stared dumbfounded at his destroyed bedsheets. They were the microfiber kind and so soft that they were almost better than silk against his skin.

Dropping the shreds, he grasped Lincoln by his hips, hauling him up over him. His cock jolted as their groins ground together by accident and Sullivan winced at the not-so-fresh feeling in his pants.

"How strong *are* you?" asked Lincoln, nuzzling into Sullivan's neck and sucking another bruise along the sensitive column. "That's so fucking sexy. I love a strong guy who can manhandle me if he wants but decides to give in to me instead."

Sullivan shuddered. And *that* was exactly what he loved. He'd been with guys who could bench-press double what he could, and he'd tried the rougher side of things, but it was nowhere near as satisfying as going to his knees for someone half his size. Lincoln wasn't quite half, but he was close enough that Sullivan dwarfed him.

He wasn't about to bring up the size difference, though. He had a feeling that Lincoln would probably take offense.

Lincoln's hard cock throbbed against him, his own insistent, despite the urge to grab Lincoln and cuddle the fuck out of him. Every bite and suck pushed cuddling a little further back on his priority list. When Lincoln dipped his fingers back into his belly button, he had a full twitch to awareness that was nearly painful.

"Can you go another round? I'm just starting to understand this whole belly button thing, and I really want to test it out." Lincoln kissed his way back down his chest, toying with the button on his ruined slacks. "I was expecting lint, but there was no lint, which is definitely a great thing."

"Yeah," said Sullivan, his eyelids heavier than he cared to admit. "Might take a bit, though. You can just fuck me if you want. I don't have to be hard for that." He usually went soft anytime something went near his ass. Not that he didn't enjoy himself, but his prostate was different than what most other men described to him. It was more of a pressure than a pleasure for him, and being full was not his cup of tea all the time.

"I'd hoped you would fuck me, actually."

That woke him the fuck up. Pushing himself upright, he nearly knocked Lincoln right off the bed in his haste. Grabbing the edge of his suit jacket, Sullivan hauled him into his lap.

"Really?" He kissed the swollen edge of Lincoln's lips. *Just when I thought I had him all figured out.*

"I may be a Daddy, but I like getting fucked. Do you not top?" Lincoln looked suddenly shy, like he had when they'd snuggled on the couch together and he'd been halfway to dreamland. His defenses were down.

"I prefer it. I just don't get to do it that often," mused Sullivan, sneaking another kiss as Lincoln looked back at him with a shocked expression.

"A big strapping boy like you? I don't believe it." He gripped Sullivan's bicep, testing the muscle with his grip. He growled as Sullivan tensed to show off.

"It's harder than you would think." Sullivan trailed off. The things that turned him on might as well have been diamonds for as often as he saw them in the wild. And dating services had led him nowhere fast when guys sent dick pics to his work phone. Samantha always had a laugh, but he was just embarrassed.

"Well, you don't have to worry about it anymore. You're mine." Lincoln surged against him, stealing his breath and possessing his mouth in the best way. Lincoln's jacket and shirt were gone a few seconds later, his and Sullivan's pants following not too far behind. They were left only in their boxers, Sullivan's clinging to him and Lincoln's barely concealing his hard cock.

Sullivan reached for him, dipping under the hem of his boxers and jerking him with a few sure strokes. He was damp, pre-cum sticking to the inside of the silk and dripping down his shaft. Lincoln was harder than steel.

"Condoms?" Lincoln asked, pulling away just long enough to get the word out. He humped against

Sullivan's hand, his cock getting slicker with each pass. "Hurry. I want you in me now."

"Shit." Sullivan reached for the drawer while doing his best not to move away at all. Sweat was slick on their bodies, the cold room doing nothing to quell the heat. Blindly, he shuffled through the drawer, his charging cable and an old iPod tumbling to the floor. Finally, he found the condoms and lube, tossing them on the bed beside them.

Wrapping his hands around Lincoln's hips, he lifted, throwing Lincoln on the bed and coming to rest on top between his spread thighs. Lincoln tossed his head back, letting out a wanton moan.

"Do you want me to?" asked Sullivan softly, taking his time to explore Lincoln's throat and chest. He settled over his belly button, saving the best for last. Dipping his tongue inside, he let out a shudder before licking the hidden bud over and over. There was nothing better than an innie.

"That tickles." Lincoln giggled, trying to pull away, but Sullivan held his hips, keeping him in place.

"It's supposed to feel good. Do you like it?" Sullivan asked shyly. He maybe had a bit of an obsession with belly buttons, but it was better than feet, in his opinion. Licking his way back inside, he tugged Lincoln's boxers down and reached for the lube.

"I think I'd like your mouth on my cock instead," said Lincoln, hissing as he was exposed to the air. He was throbbing visibly and nearly purple around the head. Sullivan winced in sympathy.

"We've already decided that you're too eager for that. Maybe next time. I want to be able to talk tomorrow." Sullivan grinned, coating his fingers with lube before sliding between Lincoln's cheeks. His hole was soft but firm, tightening up against his fingers as soon as he touched it.

"Oh, that's nice." Lincoln spread his legs, reaching to lift his sac out of the way. "Fuck me with your fingers, boy. Get me ready."

Well, that did it. If he'd doubted that he would get fully hard again, he shouldn't have worried. The second he sank inside Lincoln with one finger, his cock thrummed to life, ready to pound away for a good thirty minutes.

"You're tight and so soft for me, Daddy." He eased deeper until his last knuckle met Lincoln's rim. His entrance was stretched wide, the pucker taut as it tightened around him. His walls were like velvet. "Next time, I'm going to taste you and split you open on my tongue. I bet you're delicious."

"Just give me another. Stop talking." Lincoln threw his head back, rocking onto Sullivan's finger before sliding his own hand on his cock and giving it a few twists. "Hurry, boy, or I'll come without you, and you'll miss your chance."

He didn't need to be told twice. He pushed a second finger inside, scissoring a few times before he slowly squeezed a third in. Lincoln yielded to every touch, his walls rhythmically clenching as he bucked.

"Now your cock, boy. Come on."

Sullivan grabbed for the condom after slowly slipping out, ripping the package open and sliding it over his cock. He was still sensitive from his last orgasm, and the pressure from the condom alone was almost too much. Maybe he wouldn't last long after all.

"You want me on top or do you want to ride me?" asked Sullivan, placing a few kisses across Lincoln's belly before swirling his tongue one last time in his button. Lincoln's balls drew up with every touch, his cock dripping pre-cum.

With a hand to his chest, Lincoln pushed him until Sullivan's back hit the mattress. He jerked the pillow out from under him, bracing his heels against the bed as Lincoln climbed on board the Sully express.

There were a thousand emotions on Lincoln's face as he lowered himself, Sullivan's cock breaching his ring with a moment of surreal wonderment. There was a brief flash of discomfort, followed by disbelief and suddenly a lust that was so thick that it filled the air, tightening his chest until it was nearly impossible to breathe.

"You feel so good." Lincoln lowered himself the rest of the way, moaning as he settled at the base. His cock dribbled, a bit of pre-cum landing on Sullivan's belly.

"You rushed me when I was prepping you, Daddy," said Sullivan, barely hanging on as he started to lose himself in the pleasure and heat. Lincoln was all around him, soaking into every pore until they were barely distinguishable. "But that's okay. The first time I touch your prostate, I want it to be with my cock. I want to see you unravel as I hit your spot over and over."

Grabbing Lincoln's hips to hold him steady, Sullivan tilted his own, aiming his cock for the spot that drove most men wild. Lincoln didn't disappoint, crying out and arching his back as Sullivan aimed true.

"Daddy." Sullivan lifted him a few inches, his arms straining as he bucked into Lincoln, slamming the nerves over and over. For the first time, Lincoln seemed speechless, unable to do more than cry out and claw at Sullivan's chest.

He wasn't going to last long. *Now's my moment.*

"I have to tell you something, Daddy." He picked up his pace, cutting off anything that Lincoln had to say. The bed rocked, the headboard lightly tapping the wall. The lube bottle rolled away, thudding to the floor and probably leaking all over.

"Fuck, say it, boy, but don't you dare fucking stop." Lincoln rocked in time with each thrust, meeting every touch head-on and using his momentum to set the pace despite Sullivan's efforts.

"I'm. Not. Married." He punctuated each word with a thrust. Twisting to the side, he slammed Lincoln's back to the bed, pushing his knees to his chest. The angle let him get deeper, ramming right up against Lincoln's spot as he started to lose his rhythm. His balls were ready to empty, but he was hanging on by a thread. He needed Lincoln to come first.

Lincoln chuckled, the sound punctuated by little gasps. Grabbing the back of Sullivan's head, he gripped his hair, tugging him until his lips were against Sullivan's ear.

"I know, boy. You couldn't keep something like that from me. You're *mine*."

He couldn't take it. Thrusting one more time as deep as he could, Sullivan unraveled, emptying himself into the condom. There was an answering groan as Lincoln followed him, his cock twitching between them as he coated their stomachs. He gasped, resting his forehead on Lincoln's as his mind whirled and his body trembled.

"H-how?"

Lincoln grimaced as he glanced at the mess on his stomach, pushing Sullivan until he pulled out and rolled to his side. This time, all bets were off, and he grabbed Lincoln for the biggest snuggle of his life.

"There were a few things." Lincoln curled into his chest, placing his palm over Sullivan's pounding heart. It wasn't just the sex that was making it pound.

Lincoln leaned up on one elbow, shooting Sullivan a smile. "For one, you don't have a wedding ring, which is a pretty big giveaway. There are no pictures of your husband in your condo or on social media. The *biggest* giveaway was that Samantha mentioned how sad she was for her best friend who didn't have a boyfriend. She also mentioned he was the sweetest man on the planet."

It had all been for nothing. "Now I feel like an idiot." Sullivan hugged him tighter. He could have been doing this from the very beginning. "Why didn't you say something?"

Lincoln shrugged. "I figured you had your reasons. And it was fun to torture the fuck out of you about it."

Sullivan let out a groan, grabbing a pillowcase to clean off their bellies. His condom went next to the bed until he could manage to drag his ass out of it. "You're a little bit evil."

Lincoln's grin was predatory. "Don't you know it, boy."

Chapter Fourteen

Christmas day

"Merry Christmas, Daddy." Sullivan snuggled deeper into Lincoln's chest, his hair tickling the side of his face. At one point in the night, their positions had flipped, and he couldn't decide which one he liked better—Lincoln drooling on his shoulder and mumbling in his sleep, or Lincoln beneath him, his incessant talking finally calm.

"You too, boy," said Lincoln, ruffling his hair. "What time is it?" He stretched, his morning wood poking Sullivan in his stomach. "I don't think I've slept so much in my life."

Sullivan grinned, shifting to rub Lincoln's cock. They were naked, sweaty and a little bit sticky from the night before, but he couldn't care less. He wasn't even sure if he could get hard again, but he wasn't averse to bottoming this time. Lincoln had to be sore after a half-dozen rounds.

"Don't know. Don't care. I'm on vacation, and it's Christmas. As far as I'm concerned, we aren't leaving this bed today except for snacks," said Sullivan, sucking Lincoln's nipple into his mouth. He had to admit that Lincoln's nipples were almost on par with his belly button.

"You're getting pushy," said Lincoln, combing through Sullivan's hair. "I like it. I really do want breakfast sometime soon, though. I am dying for some carbs."

This is bliss. Lincoln in his bed, his hair messy and a silly smirk on his face was the best thing he'd ever had. None of his relationships had ever come close, even though he often fell hard and fast.

"I could probably do with some protein now, then I'll make you waffles." Sullivan shuffled down, grabbing for Lincoln's cock, which was throbbing and red. It was pretty whether it was hard or soft, but the best was when there was a pearly drop at the head. Sullivan licked it away, rolling the taste over his tongue.

"Dirty boy," said Lincoln, thrusting slowly into Sullivan's mouth.

Something vibrated on the nightstand and Sullivan looked up, his smile morphing into a glare as he saw his phone flashing and buzzing away. *There goes my vacation.* His remaining family wouldn't contact him, and Samantha was supposed to be busy, which left work.

"You have to get that?" asked Lincoln, releasing his grip so Sullivan could reach for the nightstand.

"Probably." He let out a sigh at Samantha's name. He loved his friend, but some days. "Hey, everything okay?"

The sound of sobbing had him instantly on edge, and he pushed himself to his feet, pacing away from the bed. The garbled something that Samantha was saying was impossible to interpret.

"Take a deep breath and try again, sweetie. It's okay. I'm here, and you can tell me anything. Everything is going to be fine." He couldn't remember the last time Samantha had cried—not since her relapse that had almost cost her life and their friendship.

"J-Josh proposed."

Sullivan blinked, holding the phone away from his ear for a second as he tried to process what he was hearing. That sounded like good news, not something to cry about. "Okay? Wait! You've only been dating him for three months. That seems a little quick. What do the others think about it?"

Samantha let out a wail. "I haven't told them yet. How do I even explain it to them? Josh said he's in love with me and wants to express his commitment. He doesn't care about the others."

Sullivan looked to the man lounging on his bed. The thought of another man touching Lincoln made Sullivan want to punch and strangle them, and they had only been *together* for a few days. With his monogamous ass, maybe it wasn't the speed of the relationship, but the depth of the feeling.

He really felt for his friend. There were so many people who couldn't understand having multiple partners. He just wanted her to be happy.

"It's okay. What did you say to him? Do I get to be a best man, or am I kicking someone's ass?"

Lincoln perked up, going from mildly interested to intrigued. He mouthed something that looked a lot like 'you wouldn't'. Sullivan snickered, cupping the end of the phone to block the speaker. "You might be surprised, Daddy. I'm very protective of my people."

"I didn't give him an answer. I barricaded myself in the bathroom and called you. He's already knocked on the door once to ask me to come out, but I don't know if I can alone. Can you come over?"

Sullivan bit his lip. Hopefully Lincoln wouldn't think he was using some sort of excuse to kick him out. "Yeah, I'll be there as soon as I can. I'm coming in my pajamas, though, so fair warning—and unshowered." *As soon as I find my pajamas, that is.*

"Good. Maybe you'll scare him away for me so I don't have to deal with this."

Oh, if only she knew. He was pretty sure that there was dried cum in his hair and there was definitely some on his chest. He also smelled like he'd been on a sex marathon for the last couple of days, which was pretty accurate, as far as he was concerned.

Lincoln lounged on the bed, his arms stretched over his head and his naked legs spread wide. Sullivan would have given anything to climb between them and put his mouth back where it belonged.

He shook his head as his cock perked up almost painfully, and he hung up the phone. "You up for that breakfast to go? Best friend emergency crisis."

Lincoln stretched, every hard line on display. Sullivan wiped the drool from the corner of his mouth before reaching for his discarded pajamas without looking away from the perfect sight.

"Yeah, as long as we get breakfast on the way. I'm so hungry that I might start chewing on you if I don't eat soon." He gnashed his teeth.

Sullivan's idea of grabbing breakfast on the way had been to cruise through whatever drive-through was open, but Lincoln smashed his plan to pieces yet again. Calling ahead in the car, he directed Sullivan to one of the fanciest restaurants he'd ever seen. Someone greeted them as they pulled up to the curb, running back inside and returning with a beautifully wrapped bag within a few seconds.

The smell was heavenly, and Sullivan's stomach growled as Lincoln started pulling things out of the package, beginning with an artisan bagel that honestly looked nothing like a bagel. It tasted like heaven, practically melting in his mouth as Lincoln fed him little bites.

"You want a crepe, too?" asked Lincoln, reaching into the bag. He hadn't touched a thing himself, opting to hand-feed Sullivan instead.

Sullivan nodded, keeping an eye on traffic as Lincoln fed him another bite that was soaked in some kind of citrusy syrup. Licking Lincoln's fingers, he bit back a moan. "I'm good. You can have some, too. We're almost there."

"I can wait."

They pulled up a few minutes later, but Sullivan paused before he got out, reaching over for one last bite that was followed up with a sweet kiss. Lincoln opened his mouth, sweeping his tongue against his before pulling back. "Hmmm, it *is* tasty."

Shit. Now he was hard, which his pajamas did nothing to hide. The red plaid sat low on his hips and his erection jutted out like it was searching for the Cave of Wonders, which just so happened to be located at the hottest ass he'd ever seen.

Dragging his gaze away, he marched up to Samantha's apartment building, grabbing his key from his pocket and letting himself inside. It was similar to his own place and had been built in the same year by the same company, only a dozen blocks apart. Even the little mailboxes were identical, with the crooked six on one, and a few 'return to sender' letters perched on top.

"Nice," said Lincoln, letting out a low whistle. "Modern, good looking with great accessories." He eyed up Sullivan. "I wonder who owns it."

Of course. "You know you own them both, Daddy." His own ass as well as the building. He kept his voice low, not because he was embarrassed, but because it was still early on Christmas morning. There were probably a few parents close by, hoping that their kids would sleep past eight in the morning.

The look Lincoln gave him was wide-eyed.

"Too fast?" asked Sullivan, trying to backpedal, despite the ache of want in his chest. He was getting way ahead of himself. He stopped at Samantha's door, knocking quietly against the painted frame.

Lincoln pressed against his back, touching his lips to the side of Sullivan's neck. Goosebumps burst over his skin, and he shivered in the cool hallway, his pants giving everything away. Lincoln was in a similar state, his black track pants just as effective.

Sullivan leaned casually against the frame as the lock turned in the door, setting his meanest look on his face. In his defense, it wasn't much more than a mild glare, but he couldn't do much with Lincoln practically grinding on his ass. People had run away from him with less.

The door opened and Sullivan got his first look at Josh. He'd never met him before, and it was probably a good thing, because his past self would have pined after the attractive straight man. He had nothing on Lincoln, but still…

"Who are you?" Josh pulled back, probably intimidated as Sullivan shuffled forward a step, Lincoln coming around to his side. He was sure that they looked like quite the pair—both glaring and hard—and sporting pajamas.

"I'm here for my girl. Have to give her a Christmas kiss," Sullivan drawled, rapping his knuckles on the frame when Josh didn't move. Josh's eyes went wide, and he took a half-step back.

The relationship outcome was looking dimmer by the minute. If Josh couldn't brave two other pretend love interests, then how would he compete against the real ones? Sullivan could guess exactly how, because he'd seen Samantha go through it before. She was poly through and through, which was something that someone couldn't just pretend.

"Me, too," said Lincoln, the edge in his voice much more convincing. Sullivan had to take a double look, just to make sure it was his sweet lover still beside him. The ruthless billionaire was shining through. "I'm not leaving without a piece of ass, either. Doesn't matter if it's hers or yours."

Sullivan choked, trying to cover it up with his hand and utterly failing. Josh had gone pale, clenching his hand on the doorknob and probably getting ready to slam it in their faces.

"Is Samantha here? Or are we going to have to wait all day?" asked Sullivan, crossing his arms. Josh's gaze dropped to Sullivan's biceps and he flexed, showing off every minute he spent at the gym.

"Samantha?" Lincoln whispered into his ear. "This can't get any better." Despite the excitement in his voice, his glare on Josh never wavered.

Somehow he'd forgotten that Lincoln knew Samantha, maybe better than he did. She'd told him that it was easier to write to a stranger than to talk to someone face-to-face. Lincoln was already easy to talk to...when he managed to shut up.

"Sure, come in. Sammy didn't tell me that you were coming."

Sullivan flinched at the nickname. If there was one thing that Samantha detested more than monogamy, it was nicknames. She loved to dish them out as much as she could, but she refused to shorten or sweeten her name.

"I'm not surprised, seeing as she's holed up in the bathroom." Pushing past Josh, Sullivan went straight for the bathroom, hoping that Lincoln could take care of himself for a minute. When he looked over his shoulder, he saw Lincoln pulling a muffin from his breakfast bag, taking a big chomp out of the top.

"Oh, did you bring breakfast?" asked Josh, perking up for the first time.

Lincoln leveled him with a glare. "No."

Chuckling, Sullivan knocked on the door with a few quiet raps. "Samantha, open up. It's me."

The lock clicked a moment before the door swung wide and she grabbed him by the front of his shirt and dragged him inside, slamming the door shut again. Her cheeks were streaked with mascara, her eyes so red that she looked like she'd been crying for hours. Her hair was in disarray, and she had an actual hole in her shirt.

"I think I'm gonna kick his ass," said Sullivan, wrapping his arms around her and squeezing tight. "He called you Sammy. What the hell? And he was super intimidated when we said we were here for you. It's like he's in total denial about the others. I don't want to tell you how to answer, but I think you know. I'll be here for you either way."

She let out a sob, her tears soaking into his shirt and streaking the fabric with black stains. Yeah, Josh was going down.

"He's hot, though, right?" she asked, giving him a wide-eyed look.

Sullivan shrugged. "My friend I brought along with me is hotter." Her face crumpled. "I'm kidding, Samantha, sorry. I just want to see you smile. He is hot, not quite smoking, but smoldering maybe? Piqued my interest." He pointed down to where the situation in his pants had only become a little less noticeable.

"Thought I felt the little guy," she said. "Hope that's not for me or we're both going to need therapy." A tiny giggle escaped her lips, and she gave him one last squeeze.

"You want to marry this guy?" asked Sullivan. "I'll help you pick out colors for the wedding. I just want my best friend to be happy."

She leaned against the bathroom sink, chewing her lip. "I think I would be happy...maybe for a year or so. Then he would get jealous and start insisting that I spend more time with him. He already pulled that card on Christmas. I love them all, you know, even Josh, but I don't think he gets it."

"He's not poly." Sullivan nodded. It was hard to change something about yourself that you'd been taught all your life. Sullivan had been raised in his early years thinking that everything about him was wrong and against God.

When he'd come out at twelve, his parents had left their church and had done everything they could to support him because he had been more important than their religion. Not many men he'd met had experienced something so pure.

"I think he wants to be," she said, splashing water on her face and grabbing a cloth to scrub at the mascara stains. "But from my experience, you either are or you aren't. It's not something you can change, just like your sexuality. I had just hoped…"

"Hoped that he loved you enough to change?" Sullivan filled in. His heart sank at her nod. "He loved you enough to propose, Samantha. He loves you, and he might be the only man for you — or he might not."

"Fuck, I feel so silly." She tossed the cloth to the side. It splatted against the edge of the counter, a stream of steady drips trailing onto the floor.

"Not silly — hopeful." He grabbed the cloth, rinsing it out before squeezing it and hanging it back on its hook. Samantha could thank him for it later. "You want me to kick him out?"

She shook her head, pressing her hands to her cheeks. "He's not a mean guy or anything. He'll leave if I ask him to."

He followed her out of the bathroom, waving Lincoln into the living room as she headed for the front where Josh was standing awkwardly. She gave Lincoln a curious look before grabbing Josh's hand and pulling him to the front door.

Taking a seat on the couch, Sullivan patted the spot beside him. A murmur of voices reached them from the hall, but they were too distant to catch the details.

"She going to be okay?" asked Lincoln, settling on the couch and reaching for something that looked like a fancy breakfast wrap. "The guy seemed a bit clueless. Cute, but clueless."

"I might start to take offense if you keep looking at all these other guys," said Sullivan, peering in the bag. "How much food is even in here? And what is this?" He pulled out a plastic container of something that looked like a fruit arrangement on steroids.

"Don't get jealous. I can look at who I want, but you're still my boy. I'm only fucking one person and that's you, got it? And now that we're talking about it, I expect the same from you. In a few days, we'll get tested, then I can breed up my boy like he needs."

Holy fuck. The container fell from his hand as his entire body flushed red-hot. His semi was no longer a semi, and it was not going away any time soon. He bit his lip, looking at Lincoln from the corner of his eye. "I'd like that, Daddy."

The door slammed a touch too loudly and Sullivan jumped off the couch, storming to the edge of the room. Samantha was standing by the door, looking a little worse for wear with a smile on her lips. It brightened when she saw the state he was in.

"You okay?"

"Yep," she said. "I made the right decision, that's for sure. But now you've got me wondering just what you and your ridiculously hot man are doing in my living room." She peered past him, shooting Lincoln a wave. "Hi, I'm Samantha. Sorry you had to see that shitshow."

Lincoln shrugged before waving back. "Sullivan promised me dinner and a show, and he delivered."

Sullivan choked, smacking his forehead as Samantha burst into a giggling fit. She was probably high on adrenalin and disbelief from the sound of it. She grabbed a chair and moved it to take a seat across from the couch. "You must really like this guy." She sent Sullivan a wink. "What's your name?"

It was time to rip off the Band-Aid.

"Lincoln." Sullivan swallowed, leaning against the door frame. Lincoln shot him a smirk. He was *enjoying* this.

"Cool name. I know a Lincoln, too. I think I've told you about him before, Sullivan. My pen pal."

God, she was so oblivious most days. She probably wouldn't remember her own birthday if he didn't decorate her desk every year.

"Nice to finally meet you, Samantha," said Lincoln, holding his hand out. "I always wondered how pretty you were, but I grossly underestimated reality. And this place? You told me it was a shithole. This is a nice place. I know the builders and everything."

She froze, giving Lincoln a strange look before realization seemed to dawn. Her mouth dropped open, her eyes wider than Sullivan had ever seen them.

"*My* Lincoln?" she screeched loud enough to make his ears ring. She turned a glare on Sullivan. "You knew I liked him, Sully, and you practically stole him. How did you guys even? What the fuck?"

Lincoln chuckled, offering Samantha a muffin from the bag. "This guy wrote me and told me his favorite Christmas movie, and I was so appalled that I had to call him and set him straight. Well, not *straight*, but you know what I mean. Anyway, it's all history from there."

"That's cute." She gave Lincoln a sweet smile, before pointing a finger at Sullivan. Her nail looked downright lethal. "I'm still mad at you. You stole him from me, and he's so hot." She dropped her voice, as if Lincoln couldn't hear her.

"In my defense, I don't think he's straight. He's very, very far from straight."

"You'd be right on that one," said Lincoln with a nod. "A woman can be beautiful but tell that to this guy." He gestured to his groin. "Nothing."

"Oh my God, I'm in love." She laughed, grabbing the arms on her chair. "I love a funny man. Did I tell you that?" She only had eyes for Lincoln, leaning in and showing off a touch of cleavage.

"Why do you think I've been practicing?" asked Lincoln. He relaxed into the couch, throwing his arms wide and spreading his legs in a pose that was nearly sinful. "Did I mention I'm a billionaire?"

She launched herself from her chair, darting at Sullivan. "I hate you." Her voice was a singsong, despite her words. Sometimes she acted like a thirty-year-old toddler.

Sullivan rolled his eyes, catching her and doing a spin that never failed to make her squeal. "Love you too, Bestie."

Epilogue

One year later

Sullivan rolled over in bed, wrapping his arms around Lincoln's waist and snuggling in close. Things had changed a lot since their last Christmas, but the man in his bed had stayed the same. The bed was in a different spot — in a mansion in the only part of the city that still had trees and lawns, and the sheets were silk instead of microfiber.

"Still sleepy," Lincoln mumbled, half-heartedly pushing at Sullivan before settling with a soft snort. "Merry Christmas, boy." He smiled through his sleepiness, reaching for Sullivan's head and burying his hand in his hair.

"You want to unwrap your stocking, Daddy?" asked Sullivan, squirming against Lincoln's hip. He was achingly hard and had been all through Christmas eve night. His dreams had been second to none on the sexy scale, each one better than the last.

"I'd rather stuff my stocking, boy. Come on. Get up here." He patted his lap, urging Sullivan to climb him, which he did with great relish.

There had been a time when he preferred not to bottom, but with Lincoln, nothing was the same. It was one of his favorite things to do now, besides actually fucking Lincoln. Nothing would ever top that.

"What's this?" He tapped the base of the plug that Sullivan had sneakily put inside himself just before dawn. He was slick with lube, and with a twist of Lincoln's wrist and a hefty tug, it slid free.

Gasping, Sullivan threw his head back, holding himself up so he didn't squash his lover too much. The good life had treated him well, and he'd gained a bit of muscle from his extra time at the gym while Lincoln attempted to master the highest incline on the treadmill. They got a lot of looks at the gym when they competed, both sweating and panting as they laughed.

"I already stuffed it for you, Daddy, but maybe you could put something bigger inside? I'm all ready for you and your big candy cane." Sullivan snickered as Lincoln gave him a look filled with humor.

"My *candy cane*?" asked Lincoln, slipping two fingers inside Sullivan and aiming straight for his spot. There was pressure and a flash of pleasure before he pulled back.

"Yeah." Sullivan shrugged, batting his eyelashes and going for the win. "It's big, hard, curved and I love to suck it. It must be a candy cane."

Lincoln groaned, grabbing Sullivan's hips and guiding him onto his cock. After a second of tension, his cock popped through the resistance, sliding deep inside.

Sullivan let out a groan, lowering himself to take it all. It was a lot, and the fullness was just on the right side of too much. He'd been practicing for long enough that he could almost take Lincoln without prep. *Almost.*

"I want you to fill me up good so I'm dripping all day. Be gentle, though. I'm still sore from last night," said Sullivan, letting out a few soft sighs as he started to ride Lincoln in earnest.

"Did I hurt you?" asked Lincoln, probing alongside his cock with a slick finger. Sullivan gasped, picking up his pace. Lincoln had put him through the wringer the night before, which was probably another reason that he hadn't had to use that much lube.

"No. It was so good." He hadn't been sure how their dynamic would evolve, but they were like two puzzle pieces that had always been searching for each other. Lincoln took care of him, not just physically but mentally as well, and Sullivan gave every piece of himself. "But I really want to watch that movie again."

They had been going through their movie list and Sullivan had snuck a surprise in with the others. They had only been a few minutes into *The Godfather* before Lincoln had pounced and declared that he was going to last the whole movie just to teach Sullivan a lesson.

Lincoln *had* lasted, and Sullivan's ass had suffered the consequences, not that he minded. Fucking his guy while trying to watch his favorite Christmas movie had been his New Year's resolution.

"Just because it has Christmas trees or lights in it, doesn't mean it's a Christmas movie," growled Lincoln as he rolled them over, pressing Sullivan into the mattress. "Or did you not learn your lesson last night?"

"Ah, fuck." Sullivan wiggled as his cock dribbled between them, almost as sensitive as his ass. "No lesson to learn. You know I'm right, Daddy. Now fuck me so I can give you your Christmas present."

"Fuck, boy." Lincoln picked up the pace, sucking a mark into Sullivan's neck as he writhed. It only took a few thrusts for him to come between them untouched, a skill that he was improving all the time.

"So tight for me." Lincoln let out a groan before slamming in one final time, his cock flexing as he filled Sullivan to the brim. "Shit, that was fast. Sorry. I had some pretty awesome dreams, and I was ready to go off when you woke me up."

Sullivan grinned, pulling Lincoln in for a kiss that was mostly tongue. Lincoln was still inside, cum dripping around his cock that plugged Sullivan's ass. Sullivan reached down, slicking his fingers with the mess and bringing them to his lips before leaning in for another kiss.

"Dirty boy. I love you." Lincoln sucked Sullivan's tongue into his mouth as if he were searching for every last drop.

"Love you too, Daddy," said Sullivan as he pulled back. "Now let me get your gift. I left it in the other room. Don't say that I didn't have to."

Scrambling to the other room, Sullivan tried to ignore the cum dripping from his ass, grabbing the small red bag from beneath their tree and darting back to the bed. He shuffled to Lincoln, who had rolled onto his back again. Sliding back on Lincoln's softening cock, Sullivan wiggled his hips to get situated.

"I like this gift," said Lincoln, gripping Sullivan's hips and giving a few half-thrusts. "You gonna stay like this all day for me?"

Sullivan rolled his eyes. "Only if I get my protein shake. Now shush and open your gift."

Lincoln made no move to grab the bag, tightening his grip and moving Sullivan back and forth on his cock. He wasn't even close to hard, but the sensation was somehow overwhelming. "You unwrap it for me. I'm busy."

"O-okay." Sullivan tried to blink away his desire, plucking the tissue paper from the bag. "It's a couple's gift, so we'd match if you want. I thought maybe..." He looked into the bag, losing every bit of confidence. It had looked so perfect online, but he'd developed an instant case of regret as soon as he'd hit the 'Buy' button. *What if he doesn't like it?*

"Come on, Sullivan. I know I'll like anything you got me."

Biting his lip, Sullivan tugged the T-shirt out of the bag, holding it to his chest and looking to the side so he didn't have to watch Lincoln's reaction. His heart pounded, sweat dripping down his back as Lincoln went still.

"A black T-shirt? Thanks, boy. I love it."

Sullivan looked down in confusion. The shirt against his chest was blank except for the tag that had snuck out of the collar. "Shit, it's backward. Sorry." He flipped it the right way, grimacing at the text.

"*Daddy knows best?*" Lincoln asked slowly, a grin breaking out on his lips. "Fuck, I love it! Can I wear it today? We're going to Samantha's later, and I absolutely want her to see it."

Phew. Letting out a sigh of relief, Sullivan tentatively nodded. He reached for the second T-shirt, which was the same color only with different words. "This one's mine."

"Fuck, boy, you're going to get me hard again." Lincoln surged up, crashing their lips together. Sullivan tossed the second shirt to the side, kissing back with everything he had.

"*Daddy's boy*, eh?" Lincoln bit Sullivan's lip, sucking it into his mouth and soothing the bruise with his tongue. "Don't I know it. You're the best thing I could have ever asked for. You've changed my life, and I want you in it forever. You're mine and I'm yours. Merry Christmas."

"Merry Christmas, Daddy."

Want to see more from this author? Here's a taster for you to enjoy!

Feral Woods
M.C. Roth

Excerpt

Cambry

Cambry grasped the curtain, pulling it away from the polished glass of his bedroom window. The fabric was soft and heavy in his hand — something from the latest designer his mother had fallen in love with. Instead of the previous indigo, it was now a deep blue that blended in with the softer tones of his room.

A fountain spurted beyond the window, its waters guarded by a black gate that matched the fence that surrounded the property. There were grass and trees, too, beyond those gates, not that he ever got the chance to enjoy them.

An alpha retreated along the concrete walkway, his back rippling under his thin T-shirt. Each movement was like a feral dance of instinct and desire. There was a streak of red across his shirt that hadn't been there when he'd arrived. The alpha had been big, strong, attractive and sweet — everything a proper mate should be.

But Cambry's plan had been disastrous, like a spectacular firework that had failed to launch and exploded in his face instead. The second the alpha had shown any intent that wasn't exactly platonic, Cambry's instinctive side had reared up and taken him out.

Sighing, Cambry let the curtain fall shut, the filtered light dimming to a sparse glow. Luckily, the alpha was only leaving with a scratch and a black eye instead of a broken arm like the last one—or the broken collar bone from the one before him. Maybe it was because Cambry had warned him?

Most alphas sneered at the warning—hence the broken arm and collar bone—but this one had seemed different.

"When you try to touch me, I'm going to react...badly." Cambry couldn't remember how many times he had said those same words. He guessed that the first few alphas had assumed that Cambry would react like any other omega was supposed to—with slick and a burst of pheromones.

They hadn't been expecting violence.

Walking to his dresser, Cambry pulled the top drawer wide, fumbling with a pair of boxers and tugging them up his thick legs. The fabric was smooth and silken and clutched his soft package like a fitted glove. They were worth spending his tiny allowance on, that was for sure. *Thank goodness for the little things in life.*

The little things being both his package and the expensive underwear.

His old friend Aubrie had asked him why he always splurged on the things if he had no one to show them off to. He had his own mirror, thank you very much, which added ten pounds, even on the best of days. But it was always honest about the boxers, which looked a hell of a lot better than they did on most omegas.

"Why don't you give up, Cambry? It kills me to see you like this. If an alpha hasn't induced a heat in you by now, it's not going to happen."

Aubrie had probably had the best intentions when she'd said that, but it had pierced Cambry's soul like a dull pencil crayon. Or maybe that was why Cambry's father had chosen her as his friend...to wear him down a bit more.

There was only so much loneliness he could take before he tried to be with someone again, hoping that everything would finally work the way it was supposed to. It wasn't the sex as much as it was everything else. He couldn't hug someone or even hold their hand without his feral side acting out.

His skin prickled as his door slid back, light footsteps moving across the floor behind him. And there was *that*.

"Your father is upset," said his mother, her meek voice slapping him harder than any blow. He couldn't look at her and see the same disappointment that was in his soul.

He could hear her shaking, her teeth chattering softly as she stayed as far away from him as she could. He was surprised that she had even managed to step into the same room as he was in.

"I tried, Mom," he said, pulling a second drawer wide and tugging a shirt over his frame. He had to get alpha sizes, seeing as nothing for omegas fit his frame. His father was upset about that, too.

The alpha sizes were shaped differently than he was, though—the shoulders a touch too wide and the waist not quite narrow enough. Nothing had fit him well since he'd hit puberty.

The steady thumps of his father's steps approached, and he hurriedly pulled a pair of jeans over his legs.

They at least fit a bit better, his thighs stretching the fabric to its brink as it cupped his ass. The only place with too much room was the crotch, but he was almost glad that nothing ever touched him there.

He looked at the mirror above his dresser, scowling at his reflection. Fellow omegas were terrified of him, and alphas treated him like he was a strange cousin to the human race who needed to be broken or beaten until he fit into a different shape than what he had been born into.

He sniffed, slamming the drawer shut before his father could step into his room. There was no use crying, no matter how frustrated he was.

"We've tried it your way, Cambry. These alphas can't stand to get close to you, let alone allow you to bond with them," said his father as he hovered at the edge of the door frame. He was a few inches shy of Cambry's height and had lost his alpha muscling to his age long before Cambry had been born. Like most alphas, he never got too close to Cambry—just close enough to hurt with words.

Cambry wondered if he would ever forget his father's *way*. The restraints had dug into his wrists as a strange alpha had approached him from behind. Guided by an overdressed and undereducated doctor, Cambry's father had hoped to kick-start Cambry's omega nature with some good ole fashioned alpha cock. They hadn't counted on Cambry breaking his own arm as he shifted, turning on the alpha and ripping a chunk of flesh from his throat.

The alpha hadn't died—thank goodness—but they had never tried to restrain Cambry after that. And they had finally listened to him and had let him try on his own terms by picking up an alpha from a bar. It was about as romantic as a one-night stand could have been.

But it had resulted the same way—minus the shifting and massive blood loss, at least.

"It almost happened, Dad. I was so close," said Cambry, touching his belly. He'd been naked, which had been a first. And the alpha had managed to touch him once before Cambry's beast had risen to the surface and socked him in the face. Biting the alpha's gland to bond with them had been the last thing on his mind.

"Close isn't enough," said his father, the snarl in his voice enough to prickle the hair on the back of Cambry's neck. He'd never attacked a family member, but he had come close enough times that his father rarely approached him without backup. It was probably why his mother was strategically between them, shivering with her eyes downcast.

"Your heat could kill you. You're already so much older than you should be for your first one, and there's no way you can manage it alone," said his mother, the edge of a sob in her voice. Cambry turned, his heart falling as he watched the tears stream down his mother's face. She, at least, cared for him. His father was more interested in seeing him out of the door in a different alpha's house—with some financial benefits for himself, of course.

"I'd have to *have* a heat first." Cambry turned away as his father's dark eyes glared into him. Most omegas had their first heat when they were still in high school, the late bloomers sprouting by eighteen at the latest. Cambry had turned twenty-two three weeks before, and he still hadn't experienced a heat. He was hardly an omega at all by some standards.

But his mom was right. Those that had monthly heats had the mildest cycle, still able to continue their day-to-day lives with only a mild fever and a bit of slickness. Some of Cambry's classmates had been that way, and he'd scarcely been able to tell.

Those who had heats once a year had to isolate themselves for nearly a week, their scent and instincts so uncontrollable that they could kill any stranger who attempted to approach. They *needed* a mate to ease them through it, more with their presence than their knot, from what his mother had explained.

For Cambry not to have had a heat at his age meant that his first would reduce him to nothing more than a feral beast that would kill and fuck without conscious thought. The idea was terrifying, especially since he was already so close to feral that an alpha couldn't touch him.

"I've tolerated this abnormality of yours for long enough," said his father, his mother's spine stiffening.

"Dear, you promised," she said, her voice pleading.

"No, he'll be going to *them*, and that's final. That doctor wasn't worth his degree, but a colleague of mine gave me the name of a facility that he swears by. If one alpha can't handle him, then maybe two can snap him out of this phase." He tossed a business card into the room and it fluttered end over end before settling upside down on the floor. Turning, he stormed from the entry.

Cambry finally took a breath as his father disappeared, skirting by his mother to grab the business card. It was deep forest green with the name *Feral Woods* inscribed along the middle with deep gold lettering.

He flipped it over, his eyes going wide as he read the services listed on the card. "Instinctive therapy? What is that?" It sounded terrifying and alluring at the same time.

His instincts were everything that was wrong with him, though. As much as he wanted to listen to the little whispers in the back of his mind, he knew if he did, he would be alone for the rest of his life. *Therapy* brought to mind cages and bindings, the hair on his arms and chest thickening at the thought.

If it had been his father's idea, the latter was probably exactly what was involved. His colleagues weren't much better in Cambry's experience, either.

"I hear they are very good," she said softly, her voice trembling as she took a step back. His heart broke under the weight of her fear.

His parents were terrified of him. Maybe he should be locked in a cage for the rest of his days until they found someone who could make him submit. *Or two someones.* He quivered.

"When do I leave?" He took a shuddering breath as he looked around his room. What would he be allowed to bring? His collection of rocks from his younger years? *Probably not.* His romance novels? He should probably give them a proper burial before he left, because his father would burn them and disown him if he found them hidden under the floorboard.

Just another layer of his *abnormalities*. His father would have a heart attack if he ever read one of them or even caught sight of the cover. They were the only things that Cambry had ever intentionally rebelled with, and they could cost him everything.

"Your father pulled some strings." *Because of course he did.* She cleared her throat. "You're leaving in an hour."

So his father had *expected* his plan to fail.

"There are single omegas, Mom. Why can't he just let me be?" Cambry sighed, drawing a hand down his arm as his fur retreated, prickling as it pulled back under his skin. Others described shifting as painful, and even his mother could hardly bear to do it. But to him, it was a release he only ever found when he was in that form—wild and without the presumptions of a society that hated him.

"You know why," she said, not even looking at him. He hadn't noticed the exact moment that she had given up on him, but it had been a long time ago—perhaps when he had matured into an omega, only he hadn't stopped growing like he was supposed to or maybe when the first alpha had offered him a mating contract and Cambry had bitten clear through his hand.

"I'm sorry," he said. The reasons were too long for her to list, and he knew them almost by heart. *"Your father has so much pressure at work. People are wondering why you haven't mated yet. People will talk, son, and your reputation will be ruined. We can't let them know that you're...unnatural. Your heat will kill you, and if it doesn't, your father..."*

They did have a slight point. He had no desire to die, especially since he hadn't seen the world except for his tiny slice of neighborhood and the bit of lawn within the black gates. The unmated omegas he'd seen were considered strange anomalies in the circles his father traveled in and were best to be left alone and shunned.

As if they couldn't function without a knot to drool over.

Cambry rolled his eyes. The idea of a knot made him a bit nauseous. He had no desire to bend over and *take it* like he was supposed to. His feral side agreed with toothy gusto.

"You should pack. I'll give you space." She set a duffel bag on the floor before she swept from the room, the loss of her presence barely palpable in the quiet house.

She was his polar opposite. His beast refused to be compliant and meek, even when he tried so hard to overcome that part of himself. He didn't want to be his mother, who was a shadow of a human being ruled by society more than her education and emotions.

Sighing, he looked around the room before grabbing the bag. If he were lucky, he would have just enough room to pack his books under a thin layer of clothing. Then, at least, he could take everything that meant something to him.

He looked at the business card one last time. *Alpha and omega instinctive therapy sessions. Two hundred acres of supervised development.*

Well, on the bright side, he would probably get to see some hot alpha ass. A smile tugged at his lips. He could have a positive attitude. At least he was getting out of the house. And two hundred acres would give his beast a lot more places to run, even if he was *supervised.*

Checking to make sure the coast was clear, he lifted the floorboards just inside his closet. His collection of books that he'd spent years gathering barely fit in the space anymore. The pages were worn from being read so many times, the front covers smudged from his fingers. The covers gave away everything that his father didn't need to know. Two men, bigger than even himself and twined in a primal embrace, painted a steamy picture that made his mouth water. *Forbidden Alphas.*

Heat flushed his cheeks as he packed them out of sight, zipping the bag shut with a hard pull. He balled up a pair of socks and underwear, jamming them into the side pouch to disguise the corners the books had created.

There. All packed. I hope I never come back.

About the Author

M.C. Roth lives in Canada and loves every season, even the dreaded Canadian winter. She graduated with honours from the Associate Diploma Program in Veterinary Technology at the University of Guelph before choosing a different career path.

Between caring for her young son, spending time with her husband, and feeding treats to her menagerie of animals, she still spends every spare second devoted to her passion for writing.

She loves growing peppers that are hot enough to make grown men cry, but she doesn't like spicy food herself. Her favourite thing, other than writing of course, is to find a quiet place in the wilderness and listen to the birds while dreaming about the gorgeous men in her head.

M.C. Roth loves to hear from readers. You can find her contact information, website details and author profile page at https://www.pride-publishing.com

PRIDE
PUBLISHING

Sign up for our newsletter and find out about all our romance book releases, eBook sales and promotions, sneak peeks and FREE romance books!